FAME AND FO...

David Thomas and Ian Irvine have been telling these sorts of jokes to each other for some time now. David is chief feature writer at YOU magazine, Ian is a freelance journalist. The situations in this book are not even slightly like anything that has ever happened to them.

FAME AND FORTUNE

David Thomas and Ian Irvine

FONTANA/Collins

For Clare and Jane

First published by Fontana Paperbacks 1988
© Ian Irvine and D.T. Productions Ltd. 1988

Printed and bound in Great Britain by
William Collins Sons & Co. Ltd, Glasgow

CONDITIONS OF SALE

This book is sold subject to the condition that
it shall not, by way of trade or otherwise, be
lent, re-sold, hired out or otherwise circulated
without the publisher's prior consent in any
form of binding or cover other than that
in which it is published and without a similar
condition including this condition being
imposed on the subsequent purchaser.

OBJECT OF THE BOOK

You are **Tim Tryer**, a young man in his early twenties, who has just arrived in London after receiving the benefit of a degree-level education in Media Studies and Lunch at Redbrick University. Eager to taste the pleasures denied you in your student existence, your appetite whetted by glossy magazines and TV (and by the fear of disappearing into faceless – and *Face*less – anonymity at the Jobcentre, or, worse, accountancy), you set yourself the task of achieving **FAME AND FORTUNE**.

This book provides you with opportunities to make your career in some of the various occupations the metropolis offers: currency trader, toy boy, journalist, heroin dealer, religious guru . . .

If you possess flawless judgement and are fantastically lucky you may be able to get to the happy ending of the story in a relatively short time. If, however, you are a normal human being and prone to bad decisions and worse luck it will all take a little longer. En route you may briefly taste the fruits of forbidden passion; you may enjoy unbounded wealth and suffer great misfortune; you may even die a number of grisly deaths. But don't worry about dying. **FAME AND FORTUNE** agrees with Shirley MacLaine – there really is such a thing as reincarnation.

Before you set off on your journey, here are a few tips that will make it a little easier . . .

1. Always follow the instructions at the end of every section. If you try to read the story like an ordinary book – i.e. page by page in consecutive order – it will seem like total gibberish. Of course, it may be gibberish, but that's our problem.

2. Try to remember where you have just been. Unless you are more clever than is really good for you, you are bound to get bumped off at some stage. It really helps to know where

you've just come from, so that you can retrace your steps and start again.

3. Bear in mind that what might be a sensible decision in real life isn't always the best for Tim. This is, after all, a fantasy. So live a little. Don't be afraid to be a wally – it might take you all the way to the top. And that might tell you something about the people that make it in real life too.

But now there is no time to waste. Your train is pulling in to King's Cross Station. Your future lies before you. Your pilgrimage must begin. Go to Paragraph 1 without delay. Good luck. You'll need it.

1

You arrive in London on a warm autumnal Sunday afternoon. Your eventual destination is a house in South Kensington, where you've been promised a room by an old university friend who shares the place with a selection of aspirant young Londoners. So you take the tube to South Ken and head off down the Old Brompton Road towards your new home.

It's five-thirty, a balmy sun bathes London in a golden glow and all seems well with the world. The only minor worry on your mind is that you can't quite remember the directions to the house. It's in Barchester Gardens, which is just off the next road to the left. Or is it the one after that? Or even further, perhaps?

About half-way down the block, on your side of the road, a group of neatly dressed men in their twenties and thirties are

standing chatting amongst themselves. They are all wearing expensive casual clothes – designer jeans, Italianate cotton sports shirts and leather bomber jackets. They look like the sort of trendy types who would know the area well. Perhaps you could ask them for directions?

You have three options before you. You could follow your hunch and turn left immediately in the hope of finding the house. If you think this is the best bet, turn to 43.

Or you could ask the chaps down the street if they know the way. Chat to them at 15.

On the other hand, you might prefer to trust your own judgement, carry on past the group and take one of the roads beyond them to see if you can find Barchester Gardens that way. Take this route to 102.

2

As publication day approaches, life becomes busier and busier. The press have now grabbed the story and you spend a large part of your day giving interviews and speaking to journalists on the telephone. The Attorney General wheels out various injunctions to prevent the book appearing, but with the hard work of your solicitor Toby Brief, and the legal subtlety and robust courtroom manner of your barrister OLIVER BENCHPRESS Q.C., these are overcome. The final Government appeal to the Law Lords is dismissed only three days before the book launch. First serialization rights are sold for £20,000 to *The Cursor*, 'the thinking person's binliner', which prints extracts from the book each day for a week before publication.

The morning of the launch you appear on *Start The Week* with everyone else who's puffing a book that week. Lunch finds you at ITN doing a piece on *News At One*. A phone-in on censorship on LBC completes your media exposure for the day. The launch party is held in Hawksmoor's Christ Church, Spitalfields, one of the few London buildings of architectural merit not scheduled for liquidation in your book. Indeed, it is the only building in the whole of Spitalfields not to be included in the blitzkrieg. The joint picket of the party by The Spitalfields Trust and the Georgian Group causes some ugly scenes which happily provide even more publicity when they appear on *Newsnight*.

You make your way through the meths drinkers in Princelet Street and then through the picket and into the party. *Your* party. Life is good. Go to 86.

3

You're pleased with the bike – a second-hand Czech Zcelwiczk 250cc – and pass your test in three weeks. Your leathers cost as much as the bike and you're *really* pleased with those. You don't often take them off, and people can hear you creaking at a hundred yards.

You call up Hell's Fargo, London's least prestigious transport company, and they take you on a month's trial. The job enthrals you, and you embrace the bikeboy lifestyle. Most lunchtimes you can be found in Hanover Square hanging out with your colleagues beside the telephone boxes. You stretch out in the sun on top of your machine, like a crucifixion in a Kenneth Anger movie. The work and the money soon improve your pasty complexion and run-down physique; you start jogging in the mornings and swimming in the evenings. One day as you are sprawling over your bike in your gay icon pose, feet on handlebars, hands behind head, belly button presented unashamed to the world, you are observed from a window by VANESSA FREEZEFRAME.

Go to 54.

4

You wheel yourself to the dinner-table, narrowly avoiding a Van Der Graaf generator, and meet your fellow guests:

MATT FINISH, exhibition designer and recently acclaimed for his work on *The Czeckoslovakian Tea Trolley 1919–1933* at The Crankhouse Gallery.

ARAMINTHA ARCHITRAVE, leading light in the The Gothick Society, an architectural group dedicated to the restoration and conservation of follies.

ISOBEL BASKERVILLE, commissioning editor at Hale & Hearty, recently taken over by American publishers Gateaux Schwarzwald, themselves only days ago absorbed by Lord Magnum's vast communications empire, Affair Corp.

Over the large zinc-topped table (removed from a *café-tabac* in Dijon), you settle down to a supper of grilled *chèvre* and avocado, caesar salad and *crème brulée*. The metallic surfaces make conversation difficult to hear, but fuelled by the Australian Cabernet, Kunstwerk, Finish and Architrave are very rapidly involved in an argument over the merits of Richard Branson's latest publicity stunt, masterminded by Christo. A daring piece of conceptual art was perpetrated three nights ago at 2.00 a.m. The next day Londoners found Big Ben, Nelson's Column and the Post Office Tower each wearing a giant condom.

The evening wears on. Baskerville asks you about your intentions in London, what sort of career you hope for, how much money you want to make. She is obviously leading up to something but can you handle the third large armagnac she is pouring? You meant to leave early and finish a piece for *Malice* that's getting close to deadline.

If you want to stay and find out what she is offering, turn to 132. If you want to go home, go to 27.

5

'No, thanks, I'd rather not.'

'Well, never mind, Tim. I can understand you feeling queasy about it. We'll find someone to do it. Probably Terry Tot – he'd do anything to get his byline on something marked "yuppie". What can we find for you to do? Have you ever thought about politics? We need a new parliamentary sketch writer – ANNIE SPARR has just gone for another drying-out.'

He explains the game-plan: four columns a week, 600 words a day, largely concentrating on the Question Time dogfights between the biggies, with occasional comic relief from the rude mechanicals who make up the stage army of politics.

'Just treat it as reviewing drama. Admittedly, it's more *commedia dell'arte* than Ibsen, but the essential stagecraft is there. Opening nights, overnight stars, cheers and boos, backstage gossip, comedies, tragedies, sex romps, mysteries, big production numbers, grande dames, pantomime dames, principal boy. Is it a good script, has someone been miscast, is the direction too crude, is someone hamming it up, upstaging outrageously, will this bill close after three nights?'

He offers you £500 a week for three months with a large byline. Go to 21.

6

With your heart pounding, your blood racing, and a distressing patina of perspiration breaking out across your forehead and around your body's problem zones, you stagger across the room towards Lydia. In the party's swirling hubbub conversations last no more than a moment before the tide of people carries its flotsam along to partners new. You've got one shot, one line, with which to attract Lydia's attention and make her yours.

If you're the kind of guy who'd say: 'Let me guess . . . Sagittarius?' turn to 51.

If you fancy: 'You're the most beautiful girl I've ever seen. I want to be your sex slave,' try 91.

23 gets you: 'I saw you on TV the other day. I thought you were really good.'

And at 61 you come right out with: 'Baby, I've got ten inches of prime love truncheon. Let me hit you with it.'

If you wouldn't have said anything like any of those . . . tough. Do as you're told.

7

Overwhelmed by your new status as a controversial young author, you decide to splash out. You take the delectable Rose to Oeil De L'Oiseau, a new restaurant that has caused a sensation by serving its customers frozen TV dinners reheated in a microwave and served in front of banks of televisions. The customers all sit on sofas and eat from trays perched on their knees. This gives them the agreeable sensation of running up huge expense-account bills whilst feeling completely at home.

As you sip Rumanian Riesling from plastic cups, you tuck into a 2oz 90% meat pattie with straight-from-the-freezer petits pois. Rose sticks to low-cal cod in butter sauce. You look around at the roomful of celebrities and chat-show hosts and feel that you have really arrived at the beating heart of media London.

Your good humour and confidence seem to impress Rose. Once or twice your legs brush under the table and she holds her stockinged calf next to yours for a little longer than is strictly necessary. As your eyes meet she smiles sweetly, but with an unmistakable hint of corruption.

When she offers to drive you home you know that you're on to a good thing. An invitation to coffee at her place can't be far behind. Not only is she ravishing, but she also holds the key to the TV show that sells more books than any other – what a combination.

If you sleep with her tonight, making sure to give her all your best moves, you could win her devotion and ensure that she recommends you for the *Wogan* show. But if you've misread the signs and you come on to her when she doesn't want you to, or if anything goes wrong at a later stage, you could wreck your chances all round. Perhaps a discreet goodnight at the restaurant door would be a better bet.

If you want to drive away with Rose, turn to 107. But if you don't believe in sleeping together on the first date, take a cab home to 166.

8

You and Jamie hit the white stuff with a vengeance. You've never even seen, let alone sampled, cocaine before, but it gives a totally new aspect to your disaster with Lydia. The stupid bitch, you think, how could she have been so dumb? Wow! You feel great. You could move mountains. You could make a million. Hell, several million!

So when Jamie says, 'Listen, Tryer, stop pissing around with actresses and journalism. Come to where the real action is. Times are good and hard, but we can always use some fresh blood and untainted nostrils at De B's. I could fix you a job dealing. No probs,' it's not surprising that you think: 'What a bloody champion idea.'

You could be rich. But you won't be. After three months at De Bono Lizard you have just started making serious money (and developing an even more profound accumulation of chemical addictions) when the market dips. On the principle of LIFO (last in first out) yours is the head that rolls.

Naturally the stress of such an event makes you even keener to dip your snout in some cool white snow. So by the time you get another job at Kamikaze Bank of Osaka you are well and truly hooked. As it happens the bonds into which you place $600,000,000 of KBO's reserves commit ritual hara-kiri one afternoon right in front of you on the dealing screens. You say a sad sayonara to the Japanese and try again.

To cut a long, sad story short your career is disastrous. Eventually one of your flatmates shops you to both your parents and the police. There follow a court case, a sharp fine and a prolonged stay at one of those exclusive rehab clinics for rich young junkies in the Home Counties. The cost of the court action and your detox treatment use up all of your money and most of your parents' too. You have impoverished and disgraced your family. Frankly, you can count yourself lucky that they'll have you back. Go home to Drabworthy. Stay there. And reflect on the greed that brought about your downfall. ☠

9

Your head splitting, stomach churning and forehead coated in a sheen of cold sweat, you head off in search of, first, the loo and, second, a spade. After a major session on the khazi which seems to create as many digestive problems as it solves, you venture into the garden in search of a shed full of gardening implements. The best you can do is the greenhouse, in which Lady Lymeswold has left a small wicker basket containing secateurs, shears and a small trowel. The latter will have to do to bury Labby.

Back you go to the kitchen where you steel yourself for the ordeal that is to follow by downing half a bottle of cooking sherry. 'Jusht a little hair of the dog,' you mutter to yourself, before realizing that this is not exactly the most appropriate phrase for the adventure on which you have embarked.

Labby is dragged from the kitchen, out through the back door and across the lawn, trailing doggy blood as she goes. 'This dog should be called Labby Stiffre,' you think, and then slip over onto the sodden, dewy grass, convulsed with drunken giggles at your appalling fit of humour.

Desperately, for the sun is now beginning to rise, you start hacking away at what is actually the heart of the Lymeswolds' immaculate croquet lawn. You've *got* to get the bloody beast in the ground before everyone else wakes up. You're in no state for this kind of hard labour. Your head is spinning. The world is spinning. A black cloud descends upon you.

You return to consciousness at 120.

10

The prostitutes, rent boys and their supporters begin their march with a gathering beside King's Cross. The march's start is delayed an hour while the various factions argue over who will lead. Each suggested motion has to be put to a vote of everyone present, then each vote is disputed because of the supposed bias of those counting hands, then it is questioned whether everyone who voted was entitled to vote. The line-up is finally decided when the transvestites and prostitutes combine against the lesbians and rent boys, who are unable to offer enough concessions to the one-parent families to bring in their block vote. The other smaller groupings fit in where they can after these. A banner declaring 'Manchester Adventure Playgrounds Against Sexism' brings up the rear.

You march along with Gay Bikers For Peace and join in their chant: 'HO- HO- HOMOSEXUAL, CAPITALISM IS IN-EFFECTUAL.' A six-foot-six black-leather-clad biker wearing a moustache, a lot of chains and a tee-shirt with 'Lavender Menace' written on it offers you a fruit pastille. You notice wool, knitting needles and a half-finished baby jacket protruding from his pocket.

Because of the earlier delays, the Christian Purity League have already arrived at Trafalgar Square and occupied the platform around Nelson's Column. They have around four thousand supporters. The more eclectic bunch you're with muster around twelve thousand and are pouring into the square rapidly. You decide that you've got enough grass roots material for your piece and withdraw to the terrace of the National Gallery for a clear view of the expected punch-up. There you find Johnny talking to an attractive woman in her thirties with a film crew. He introduces you to VANESSA FREEZEFRAME, well-regarded TV producer, currently working for Obscure Opinions, the radical independent programme makers. Go to 101.

11

Stand and fight? Against this lot? You must be out of your mind. Custer faced better odds at the Little Big Horn. You will, however, have little time in which to regret your decision. The Blue Moon Defective Agency descends upon you like hyenas on a wounded lamb. Their knives flash in the evening sun. Their chains whistle through the air towards your unprotected scalp. Exotic Oriental weapons, with razor-sharp blades and cruelly honed spikes materialize in their hands. Before you can cry out, they have sliced and diced you with all the immaculate precision of a team of formation *sushi* chefs. You die on the pavement, your life bleeding away into the gutter, just another statistic lost in the rising tide of urban crime. When the police come to take away your lacerated corpse they find a vellum card pinned to your chest. The following words are printed on it, embossed in gold: 'Congratulations. You are the latest client of the Blue Moon Defective Agency. We trust that you have enjoyed the experience.'

If it's any consolation, the peculiar savagery of your demise earns you a little notoriety. Several MPs call for your killers to be hanged, but they are never found. *The Sun* sums it up best: ANIMALS CARVE UP MAN FOR DINNER. ☠

12

The kitchen is still warm from supper but cooling rapidly. You find a half-full bottle of Scotch and take some swigs to warm you up. You open all the drawers, emptying most of the contents over the floor, and eventually find three large tablecloths. You wrap yourself in these and snuggle down on the kitchen floor against the Aga. It's not very comfortable, but you feel certain you're not going to freeze to death. You finish the whisky just to make sure and rapidly lose consciousness.

During the night you have a terrible nightmare in which you are being crushed by an enormous grizzly bear. Its horrible slavering jaws are beside your ear, the smell is appalling. You are soaked in sweat and straining hard but you can't escape. With a final great effort you burst free and a stick appears by magic in your hand. With one blow you crown the grizzly who vanishes with a horrible moan.

Your heart soon stops beating 180 to the minute and you sleep easily for the rest of the night. Go to 105.

13

It just gets better and better. You and Darren keep on knocking out great creative concepts for the Flavoured Condom account and you feel honour-bound to try out the product on most of the secretaries in the office. You scallywag.

Eventually the lemon, orange, strawberry and passion-fruit johnnies are ready to be launched under the slogan; 'Give 'em something fruity for afters.' The party to celebrate this milestone in British sexual and gastronomic history is to be held at the Café Madrid, an old jazz-age nightclub recently restored to its former glory.

It's been a hard week, it's Thursday evening and there's a great old Howard Hawks movie on Channel 4. On the other hand, you really should go to the launch. If you feel like staying in, mooch back to Barchester Gardens at 103. But if you reckon a night on the town might be just the sort of bracing tonic you need, groove along to the Café Madrid, currently located at 35.

14

'You bastard!'

C. U. Incourt's pink cheeks, already flushed with Hock, are further inflamed by your revelations about the bishop's daughter, which you relate in rather crude terms. Unfortunately your informant failed to tell you that Cicely Toogood's young man was a journalist, indeed a diarist, in fact, the very man whose wine you were until a few seconds ago affably drinking.

After delivering a freezing warning to you and Johnny about the consequences of spreading this slander, Incourt picks up his astrakhan-faced overcoat and leaves El Vino's by the side-door.

Johnny regards you morosely – you have cost him one of his best Fleet Street contacts. However, to make the best of this debacle he suggests that you could still sell it to one of the Sunday scandal-sheets. They pay big money, he says. Do you approach *The Ooze of the Globe*? If so, turn to 28. If you want to drop it and go home, turn to 176.

15

You walk up to the nearest man of the group and ask the way to Barchester Gardens. He seems unwilling to tell you and when you ask him again he becomes abusive. Very, very abusive. As he peppers you with adjectives beginning with 'f' and nouns beginning with 'c' his breath hits you with an evil blast of whisky, extra-strong lager and vindaloo. One sniff of this disgusting emission is enough to induce toxic shock, and its ingredients have already done some pretty intensive work reprogramming, downgrading and mutating the contents of your interlocutor's head. He is, to be short, as pissed as a newt. And so are all his mates. What's more, the acute perceptiveness that you regard as your major asset as a writer-to-be has also told you something else. These guys are not only pissed, but pissed-off. They're angry and they're looking for trouble. Quick, keep moving, turn the next corner and run like hell to 67.

16

You wake up with a start. Four figures are crouched around you. They are dressed in Eastern robes. Their faces, curiously, like their clothes, are blue. By chance you have been discovered by members of the Kashmiri sect Utta Rabbash, who venerate the colour blue and paint their faces with it. They are overwhelmed to discover the world's only blue-skinned human.

Over the next six months your life improves considerably. You live in the Rabbash ashram in Brighton and find that continual veneration does a lot for your self-esteem. Eating only blue vegetarian food does cause problems, but the change of diet does seem to clarify your ideas. You start writing down your thoughts on blueness.

Another six months and your life has taken a dramatic shift. Your book of meditations, *Come On You Blues*, has become wildly popular. Converts are flocking to your ashrams and donating their personal wealth to the Azure Foundation. Many of these spiritually impoverished (but materially over-endowed) people you met in 'your earlier life': Sophie Godyah-Raleigh is an early follower. She becomes part of your group of close female acolytes: those who have considerable potential for spiritual growth, who have seen through the vanity of the world and have great legs.

Three years later and the harmony of your existence has been unbalanced by impertinent investigations by the IRS and FBI of the Azure Foundation's activities in the United States. They have seized your thirty-eight blue Rolls-Royces and Cadillacs. Your worldwide following of 22 million still have faith in your Blueness.

While passing through London secretly you stay at Barchester Gardens, now renamed Centre For The Future Blue World (Sophie gave it to you when she first became a follower). You see a group of blue-clad people outside and go out to allow them to kiss the hem of your robe. Unfortunately you are beaten to death by these Chelsea fans on their way home from a particularly depressing 4–nil loss to Stoke City.

Fame, fortune, beautiful lovers – you had it all. What shall it profit a man if he gain the whole world and still be unable to identify a bunch of psychopaths outside his door? Think about it.

17

You are excited to meet these authors whom you have admired since school when you were encouraged enough to keep a journal of your sixth form trip to Brussels. It was published in the school magazine as 'Flanders And Swanning Around'.

You visit F. T. Comment in a chaotically untidy cottage in Suffolk. He is much younger than you imagined, probably early thirties. After pouring large whiskies for everyone in the film crew he gives you amusing anecdotes of the Indian journeys described in *Pith In My Helmet* and the East African explorations soon to be published in *A Very Standard Bearer*. The interview is interrupted when the rain clears at Edgbaston and the Test Match continues. Comment sits in front of the television until another cloudburst stops play. After filming he takes you all down to the local pub, The Questing Vole.

In his Campden Hill flat, Stanislaus Nuristan, half-Polish, half-Punjabi, completely homosexual, recalls the 1930s in Afghanistan. This friend of the Sitwells has just published an intense passionate memoir, *Up The Khyber*.

You manage a brief dialogue with Ingrid Reference in her suite at the Savoy Hotel; she is passing through on her way between her flat in New York and the one in Paris. This small, chic, neurotic Bostonian wears dark glasses throughout. She laconically tells you how she wrote *Tiger Rag* about Sri Lanka's civil war with the Tamils while being too frightened to ever leave the Colombo Hilton.

Now that these interviews are in the can, what are you going to do with them? You could do a straight report, using the best anecdotes and presenting these first-class authors you admire in a good light.

Or you could be brutally unfair, using out-takes from the filming and sarcastic voice-over comment to send up your interviewees as writers and people.

If you want to be Mr Nice, go to 96. If Mr Nasty, 44.

18

C.U. briefs you on the BBC story: how the rising young Controller of TV Light Entertainment found himself relegated to Deputy Head of Welsh Language Broadcasting. He tells you to get in touch with comedy writer PETER PUNCHLINE, who knows all the details. You finally manage to catch him at the Radio 4 studio of *Midweek*, where he is plugging the just published book of scripts of his most famous sitcom, *Pick Up The White Man's Boudin*, a story of three West Indians starting a French provincial restaurant in Southport. He says he'd prefer not to talk on the phone. Are you free for a drink round lunchtime?

You meet at The Knob and Dial pub behind Broadcasting House where, over eight gin and tonics (him) and four Pils (you), he relates a sordid tale of sex, ambition and memos, involving ebullient Scouse producer LAURA LAFFS and career grey man NORMAN HORNRIM.

After you've got the story you remind Punchline that you've met him before, when he addressed your Media Studies Group at Redbrick University. He remembers, and tells you how amused he was by the brilliant academic parody you pressed on him then. (In fact you gave him your finals' thesis, 'The Plain and the Spotted: A Structuralist Approach to The Woodentops', which you still take very seriously.) His current project is a new comedy series, *Not Waving But Gargling*, and he's looking for ideas. He asks you to come and see him next week in his office at Television Centre.

Take the tube to White City on 100.

19

The giant pharmaceutical firm Pill Corp have been understandably wary of bad press since the early Seventies when a BBC documentary revealed that six of their top brands had identical formulas. Before their tame medic TIM ORR-MORTICE will give you the new Yuppie Flu treatment, still in pre-market testing, you have to sign sheaves of legal documents absolving Pill Corp from all responsibility. Now if they inject you with cyanide and you die on the spot, your parents will probably have to pay them compensation.

The treatment begins with a series of excruciating injections, but within hours you begin to feel considerably better. Within a few days your depression has lifted, and you can manage to get about. You feel fitter and much healthier and you seem to be getting some colour back in your cheeks . . . the problem is that it seems to be blue. The depression returns.

Over the next week it becomes certain: Cumulus, Snowbell, Hydrangea, Delphinium – the Dulux paint charts mark your gloomy progress. Have you got the blues. Lupin, Jay, Sahara Twilight . . . With some more faint-away injections Dr Orr-Mortice manages to stabilize your condition and even add a little green.

At last, Port Arthur Blue – would you rather have the Yuppie Flu symptoms? – well, you don't have the choice. You feel fine physically. Mentally you are a paranoid wreck.

Since, apart from the unfortunate skin tone, there is now nothing wrong with you, the hospital discharges you. Go to 55.

20

A late paid cheque for expenses arrives giving your bank balance a healthy £500. This could be your chance to get out of the rut. What are you going to do with it?

If you want to put it towards a motorbike and gear, so that you can become a bike messenger, rev up on 3.

If you want to invest it in the latest share issue in the government's privatization programme, British Prisons, fill in the application form at 41.

If you want to start dealing in heroin for your building, buy your supply from your friendly smack wholesaler at 58.

21

Life at the House of Commons soon settles into a pleasant routine. One morning two months later is just like any other: you gently pick through the day's newspapers after breakfast. Mid-morning you arrange to have lunch with yet another backbencher with a majority of 12 in the last election, desperate for a mention in the press to increase his public profile. After lunch you stroll to the press bench in the chamber and cast a satirical eye over the monkey-house. It's just as Terence Broadsheet described it – though possibly more Theatre of the Absurd than *commedia dell'arte*.

You file your copy (500 words poking not so gentle fun at the Junior Minister of Situations) from the press room at 5.30 and work is over for the day. Two invitations are open to you: a drinks party at the Ministry of Defence to celebrate the delivery of a new battle tank, or a product launch at the Café Madrid (courtesy of a newly appreciative Terry Tot).

Tankies at 165. Trendies at 35.

22

Stop playing silly buggers. This is a wardrobe we're talking about here. What happens if the person who owns the bedroom it's standing in decides to move house? All of a sudden you could find your home being moved to a delivery van or sitting in some warehouse somewhere. Don't do this to yourself. Go back to 46 and choose yourself a proper home.

23

What a wimp. Sycophancy may get you a flicker of interest from Lydia, but it'll never inspire the kind of feelings in her that you want to evoke. Go to 161 and try your luck again there.

24

Des Res Developments have their headquarters in Mayfair, just off Grosvenor Square. This is your first visit to Des's place of work – when you interviewed him it was in the mansion in the super-plush Surrey suburb of St George's Hill, shared with his new wife, a twenty-one-year-old model called KELLY-MARIE. Des may favour concrete and plastic for his developments, but his office is ostentatiously traditional, with heavy oak panelling on the walls and carpeting as deep as elephant grass.

'Come on in, Tim me old son . . . awntray, awntray.' Behind his bonhomie Res, a bulky man in his mid-fifties, still retains some of the sense of menace that made him light-heavyweight boxing champion of the Marines during his National Service days. He started with a couple of derelict buildings in the Old Kent Road, managed to offload all his tower blocks and shopping centres ahead of the collapse in 1974, and is now making a second vast fortune out of the twin City and domestic booms of the 1980s.

By way of introduction you admire the panelling. 'Yeah,' he agrees, 'a lovely bit of wood, that. Came out of a country house we converted into a conference facility. Put up some plastic veneer instead. No one notices. They've only gone there to get pissed away from the wife.'

Then he gets to the point. 'I've been in this game a long time, Tim. I've been everywhere and I've seen it all. But this is a young man's business now and I'm looking for people who'll run the show when I decide to devote a little more time and attention to my Kel. Now, you're a bright lad and you've got a way with words. I can use that. Presentation is what it's all about in property. You've got to sell yourself to the authorities to get planning permission. You've got to sell yourself to your clients to make a profit. Are you with me?'

Absolutely, you reply. So move on to 84 to hear the rest of what he has to say.

25

You marry the Hon. Camilla Something in the chapel at Whatnot Hall on a perfect, crisp October day. The whole of high society attends and many of the younger ones are, indeed, high all day. Your flatmates are hugely impressed by your new status. A few weeks ago you arrived penniless and obscure on their doorstep, now here you are being helicoptered from the lawn of your father-in-law's stately home en route to a honeymoon at the family's cottage on Mustique.

On your return Lord Whatnot installs you in a delightful house in Holland Park and arranges an agreeable job for you at Cholmondley's, the merchant bank of which he is a major shareholder. You are the firm's first-ever non-Etonian employee.

Surprisingly, your marriage to Camilla flourishes. As is often the way with wild, titled girls, she settles down into entirely conventional motherhood. Sophie's step-father Sir Nicholas Lymeswold marks you down as a coming man and his influence, combined with the shadowy presence of Lord Whatnot, ensures that your banking career is paralleled by a steady rise through the ranks of the Conservative Party.

In time you inherit Sir Nicholas's safe county seat. With Camilla and your four children at your side you ascend to ministerial rank, only to be brought down by a particularly steamy sex scandal. *The Ooze of the Globe* (by now edited by Johnny Standfirst) leads with: 'SHAME OF TOP DOG'S DODGY DOG-LOVING' – a torrid tale of the Rt Hon. Timothy Tryer MP's intimate association with a German Shepherd called Duke. The dog becomes a celebrity, the *Ooze* puts a quarter of a million on its circulation, and you retire in disgrace to a villa in Tuscany, with only the consolation of a substantial kennel.

This was not the FAME AND FORTUNE you sought. If your old ambitions still remain, try, try and try again. ☠

26

You turn up at TV Centre two minutes before airtime wearing oily mechanics' overalls, combat boots and a black beret. In your right hand is a bottle of whisky. In your left a Kalashnikov rifle.

Rose is appalled. But, shoving her out of the way, you swagger onstage while Wogan is still in the middle of his introductory monologue. With commendable professionalism he manages to make your appearance look deliberate, guides you to a chair and begins the interview.

In response to his first question you spit on the floor, take a swig from the bottle, put a bullet in the ceiling, call the divine Tel a fascist bastard and tell him he's lucky his own home and family aren't on the demolition list.

When he tries to calm you down and attempts a soothing pat on your knee, you karate chop his thigh and wander off to insult the studio audience. By now the place is in uproar, which is only increased as armed para-military police burst into the studio to arrest you.

No one will forget your television debut, that's for sure. It was more violent than Rambo and more embarrassing than the elephant that crapped on *Blue Peter*. Rose is furious and ashamed to have recommended you. 'I never want to see you again,' she screams as you are led away.

In the end you get five years in jail. Go to 119.

27

You finally find a minicab back to Barchester Gardens. Black coffee and nicotine fizzing in your bloodstream, you manage to complete your piece on self-made teenage millionaires for *Malice*.

You wake fully dressed with your nose in your portable typewriter. More strong coffee kickstarts your brain and you deliver your article to Charlotte Van Dryver personally at 8.30, when she arrives fresh from her tai-chi exercises and eighteen lengths of the swimming-pool at John Brown's Body Studio, Mayfair. Over the croissants flown in from Paris to *Malice*'s office, you read the mail that has arrived at the office for you since your left-hander feature.

There's an interesting letter on *The Cursor* headed paper from Terence Broadsheet. He invites to lunch and you decide to accept. Go to 48.

28

Johnny Standfirst makes a phonecall to his contact DUD FIVERS and you set off. *The Ooze Of The Globe* has recently moved its offices from Fleet Street to a high-tech establishment in London's Docklands. However, the area's lack of infrastructure (i.e. no pubs) has meant that the more 'creative' of the staff never go there, preferring to send their copy down the telephone with a portable computer. Fivers is discovered in South London at a very *folklorique* pub, The Blind Referee, off the Old Kent Road. Ronnie the barman sets you all up with Scotches and you outline your salacious story to the attentive hack. Fivers is very keen and says he thinks his paper could pay you £5,000 but only if you are willing to set up a meeting with the pair of lovers, so that the paper can secretly photograph them.

This means you will become a moral leper when it becomes obvious that you shopped them. If you want to go ahead, turn to 53. If you want to forget the deal and go home, go to 176.

29

The theatrical party is being held in a private room at The Groucho Club, a sort of not-quite-Garrick Club for upwardly aspirant media, publishing and showbiz types, located in the high-chic Soho environs of Dean Street. As you pass through the main bar on your way up to the party, you see a brilliant young fashion designer. He is wearing shorts. With him is a face you vaguely remember from a picture by-line in a Sunday supplement style feature. It is TERRY TOT, the brilliant fourteen-year-old style pundit whose word is law in the world of fashion-consciousness. He too is wearing shorts. You begin to wonder whether your trousers aren't rather passé.

Sonya leads you upstairs and you go in to the party. It is a sea of familiar faces. At first you think that you know almost everyone there. Then you realize that it's just that you've seen them all on TV. Slender, elegantly dressed young men are whispering into each others' ears and then chuckling with catty, conspiratorial laughter. Grizzled agents are talking percentages with dizzy blonde actresses who have little girl eyes and minds like calculators. Fragments of conversation float across . . . 'So then Andrew said to Sarah' . . . '$200,000 a week – *profit*' . . . 'of course, she's always had *talent*, but can she act?'

With a vague wave Sonya cries, 'Ciao, darling. I must just circulate. Enjoy yourself,' and disappears. What will you do? Find out at 126.

30

Very possibly the best thing available on the menu, but a dangerously banal choice, redolent of Berni Inns and Spanish resort holidays. Remember, in Britain the 'best' restaurants are not just places where you can have a decent meal (quite often they are not *even* places where you can have a decent meal), they are yet another way of demonstrating social status and parading conspicuous consumption. The trappings of the establishment, the decoration, the address, the service, the celebrity of the chef, the celebrity of the diners, the fashionability, novelty and expense of the dishes and wine all come before the unbearably simple question: Is the food any good?

You recover your cool in Miss Van Dryver's eyes, however, with a long and amusing Structuralist analysis of the 'meaning' of Parma ham and steak and chips as cultural icons: rather putting the Barthes before the horseradish.

Move to 112.

31

It takes two hours to photocopy the manuscript. You lug back the three copies and the original to Barchester Gardens. The sinister observer has disappeared; you're not worried any more now you have more than one manuscript. You call your editor Isobel Baskerville and get her to send a bike round for one. It feels as if you had just given birth. 'My baby, my baby,' you croon, stroking the pile of sheets.

You have written the book in three months; however, it takes the publishers six months to get it into the shops. In the meantime you keep your writing career going with pieces for *Malice*: Yuppie Flu, Fashionable Welshmen, and a series of profiles of exiled royalty (you collect an assortment of medals and memberships of orders including the Sash of Chastity, the Carpathian Cummerbund and Grand Commander of the Lavender Lapel. The amiably deranged Emperor of Haiti creates you Earl of Mango).

A month before publication Isobel Baskerville calls you at 9.30 p.m. She sounds worried and wants to see you the following morning for an urgent meeting at Hale & Hearty. Go to 151.

32

Sad to say your big break never broke. Or, at least, it just broke down. *A Kick Up The Arts* lasts a mere two transmissions. Its radical opinions are just a teensy bit over the top for the IBA who, in addition, are leaned on heavily by the Home Office. Perhaps it wasn't such a good idea to showcase the radical performance artist whose act consisted of offering £1 million, cash, to be deposited in a Swiss account, to anyone who assassinated the Arts Minister. The contract with Channel 4 is terminated with extreme prejudice. Special Branch raid the production office.

Libel writs are then brought against the show by Auberon Waugh, Clive James, John Mortimer, Richard Ingrams and Michael Grade. As the presenter who actually made most of the libellous remarks, you are named in the writs.

The controversy is immediately taken up by the tabloid press who cast you as a crazed left-wing menace to society. Measures are set in hand to have you named as a man unfit to be allowed on the airwaves in a special amendment to the Broadcasting Act. Paul Johnson devotes a leading article to you in the *Daily Mail*. The other inhabitants of Barchester Gardens – fed up with the reporters camping by the front door and going through the rubbish – ask you to leave. You'd better lie low for a while. Go to [152].

33

Perhaps it's your Drabworthy upbringing, but you've always believed in the philosophy of 'safe not sorry'. All this rushing off to New York at a moment's notice sounds like rather too much of a good thing. Much better to stay in London and see what transpires. Doubtless Nelson Ratings will still be around in a year or so if you ever change your mind.

So on Wednesday morning, instead of rushing round to the American Embassy for a visa, you phone Peter Punchline at the BBC. He invites you for lunch later in the week. Go off to see him at 100.

34

Your first stop is the Aerodrome – a hi-tech, low-taste London nightclub where The Idle Rich are rehearsing, or attempting to do so, for their performance that night. Sadly, their innate inability to grasp such concepts as 'professionalism', 'punctuality', 'organization' and so forth – their suspicion that these ideas reek of trade and are thus beneath them and too, too boring for words – has meant that few of the band are present.

The singer is off shopping in Bond Street, the guitarist is trying to track down first his dealer and then his tailor, and the horn section have all gone hunting with the Quorn. Never mind, as the club owner, Welsh impressario DAI ICE explains, The Idle Rich are just what you're looking for.

The group's eleven person line up is like a roll-call from Debrett's mixed with an inmates' reunion from the country's finest private drying-out clinics. The only untitled group member – one of three female back-up singers – is rumoured to have slept with all three of the Queen's sons and is the heiress to a vast bathroom accessories fortune. Of the rest, there is an Earl, three Viscounts, two Lords, an Hon., plus the daughters of two Dukes and a Marquess. The latter, LADY MIRANDA MOUNTEBANK, has already earned considerable acclaim in the tabloids, for such exploits as motorcycling topless through Knightsbridge and putting LSD in the tea at a Buckingham Palace garden party (many of the guests joined Prince Charles in earnest conversations with the azaleas). These jolly japes have earned her the soubriquet of Mad Miranda. You have come prepared with the first line of your piece. 'Miranda Mountebank may be a Lady. But she's no lady.'

That's as may be, but when she finally sashays into the Aerodrome, laden down with bags from Crolla and Chanel, it is immediately apparent to you that Lady Miranda is one of nature's stars. She looks dark, sulky and spoiled. Her mouth is a scarlet pout, her slender body is clad in tight, black leather. She is clearly horny beyond belief and outrageously desirable. This girl could be mega. Damn, you'll have to change the whole tone of your piece.

As the day goes by, the rest of The Idle Rich turn up. You see their show that night and manage to have yourself invited to their next gig – a twenty-first birthday party for Camilla Something's sister Clarissa at Whatnot Hall. By now you have got to know the group well and they are hugely impressed by your ability – almost unique in their experience – to remain sober and straight for several hours at a stretch. And your enthusiasm for Miranda's talent and suggestions as to how this might best be projected are warmly received. After the Whatnot show, Miranda and her boyfriend VISCOUNT FENDER, the bassist, suggest in a casual sort of way that you might be interested in managing them. Clearly they see this as a role somewhere on a par with that of a junior gamekeeper. But you can see that Miranda Mountebank could become a sort of Lady Madonna – in fact, now you come to think of it, you could even promote her that way – and that 20% of the band's potential earnings would be an extremely tasty prospect.

Should you accept this generous offer? If you can't resist, turn to 167. But if you'd rather remain a journalist, thanks all the same, go no further than 125.

35

Wow, is this place trendy, or what? The velvet banquettes and gilded passageways of the Café Madrid are stuffed to bursting with London's dandiest denizens. The boys wear torn denims, cycling gear, black polo necks and little caps on the backs of their heads. The girls all wear dresses that are short and black. The radical ones team these with heavy boots, cropped hair and aubergine lips. The bimbos go for stilettos and bleach blonde cuts like a hundred shag-pile carpets. A prominent fashion editor is taking notes. He is wearing a crisp Chanel skirt suit, a pussycat bow and hair like Oscar Wilde, but not so butch.

Up to you comes TERRY TOT, the dynamic, shorts-wearing, fourteen-year-old style columnist. He is immensely impressed by your recent run of success and greets you in the brusque tones he employs to disguise the fact that his voice has yet to break. 'Tim. Hi. How's things? I hear you're a happening guy these days.'

You reply that things seem to be going well.

'Hey, listen,' says Tot. 'Got a great idea. Come and have dinner. I'm grabbing some Chinese with a couple of white Rastas. It's going to be well crucial.'

Now that you're committed to a night on the town, you might as well go for it. Hit the Peking Duck at 81.

36

Camilla is hugely amused by your description of the dinner as a party game, possibly because she is already half-cut herself (the considerable quantity of illegal narcotic substances she consumed while dressing for the party didn't hurt either). In no time at all you're getting on like a house on fire. It seems she has a flat in Princess Diana's old block, Colherne Court. It's just round the corner from Barchester Gardens.

By now you can see that Sophie is making considerable progress with Hamish. Clearly the two of you will not be making your way back home together tonight. But Camilla offers you a lift in her Renault 5 Gordini and you gratefully accept.

You have never known the true meaning of fear until you have spent twenty minutes in the passenger seat of Camilla Something's car. As the stereo pounds out Terence Trent Darby she does 65 miles-per-hour up the wrong side of the Fulham Road, plays chicken with a double-decker bus, all-but runs down two cyclists and an old-age pensioner and finally deposits you, trembling uncontrollably, outside her mansion block. When she invites you in for coffee you are too stunned to resist.

Her flat is a tip. Record sleeves, Rizla papers, empty bottles and overflowing ashtrays litter her drawing room. When you go to the bathroom for a pee it is strewn with drying knickers and tights. The entire kitchen is covered in a thin layer of dust and penicillin mould.

By now it is quite clear that the Hon. Camilla is a dangerous proposition. She's clearly game for anything, however, and the prospect of a night with the daughter of one of the country's leading peers is an enticing one. Should you take your chances and stay with Camilla at 118, or go home to bed at 129?

37

The men from Mounting and Joist appear on the appointed day and look at your home in contempt. They ring up their guv'nor to check that they've come to the right place and seem peeved to be told that they have. These are men who have worked on mansions in Mayfair, castles in Kent, fancy flats in Fulham, and here they are now, relegated to a piss-hole in Poplar.

But they're professionals, so they get to work. After a couple of days one of them approaches you. 'Did you have this place surveyed, then?' Yes, you say, you did. 'So you know it'll need new foundations and complete underpinning?' No, you damn well did not know that. Nor were you aware of the fact that many of the little details of finish that you request were not in the original estimate and will have to be charged as extras.

The weeks go by, the costs pile up. You get the damage at 114.

38

You tiptoe along the first-floor passage in the dark – you're sure that Victoria is in the last bedroom on the left. You stop at the door and listen. There is some noise from inside – good, she's still awake and moving about. You rap very gently on the door. The noise inside stops and you hear Victoria's voice saying, 'Ollie, what was that?' A male voice boozily replies, ''sjust Labby prowling about.' The noise inside begins again.

You tiptoe away, feelings of jealousy, frustration and embarrassment seething in your rapidly chilling breast. Your steps lead unsteadily towards the kitchen at 12.

39

You idiot. You've given them exactly what they wanted – an excuse to give you an even bigger hiding than you would have had anyway. They hammer you mercilessly. The hospital doctor who sees you after a night of agony in the cell into which you were eventually thrown, will report a terrible assortment of contusions and broken bones.

The worst damage you managed to inflict on your opponents was a couple of black eyes. Not much, but enough to ensure that charges of assaulting police officers stand a much better chance of sticking than they might otherwise have done. When combined with further charges of breach of the peace, behaviour likely to cause an affray, drunk and disorderly conduct and – last but by no means least – gross indecency, they make an instant criminal record any yob could be proud of.

It goes without saying that you lose your job. When you come to trial few of your former friends will come forward to act as character witnesses. Eventually Johnny Standfirst speaks on your behalf because he is both politically sympathetic to alleged victims of police brutality and also constantly in search of good material for stories. And Sonya Stagestruck vouches for your apparent heterosexuality (she has no first-hand experience of it, but she is prepared to believe you) because her agent has told her that an appearance as a beauty in the witness stand never hurt any aspiring actress.

The two of them do much to persuade the judge and jury that you have, until now, been a decent sort of chap, unlikely to have made a habit of exposing himself to unknown men in dark alleys. And the court also feels that it is unlikely that injuries as extensive as yours could have been brought on entirely by necessary restraint or self-infliction. But you have, it is generally agreed, obviously behaved badly and society is generally best kept protected from obnoxious, violent drunks, particularly in these times of rising crime rates and general decline of public standards.

You are found guilty on several counts pertaining to alcohol and violence. The judge, stung by the recent press reaction to his sentence of one hundred hours of community service to a child molester and rapist who happened, it later transpired, to belong to his Freemasons' lodge, sends you down for seven years. As he does so he expresses the hope that the severity of the sentence will act as a deterrent to other middle-class young men inclined to forget the responsibilities imposed on them by their privileges.

Go straight to jail. Do not pass 'Go'. Do not collect £200. Your cell awaits at 119.

40

Lydia's chin rises, her clear blue eyes turn to ice as she looks down her perfectly chiselled nose. Her nostrils wrinkle slightly, as if assailed by an as-yet unidentified, but infinitely unpleasant smell. Finally, in a low, venomous voice she speaks: 'Why don't you crawl back under your stone, creep?'

Then she turns on her patent leather heel and walks away, leaving you for dead.

A few other guests have witnessed your humiliation. Silence falls across the room and then is replaced by a buzz of bitchy chatter. 'Really, Sonya, where *did* you find it?' a man is asking, entirely unconcerned by the fact that you can clearly hear him. You have no choice but to leave, but where will you go? The night is still very young. Johnny won't have come off his shift yet and Sophie's social arrangements are clearly so chaotic that no one will mind if you do turn up with her after all. Alternatively you could go home and lick your wounds with a bottle of booze and the telly.

Johnny's at 79, Sophie's dinner party at 138 and Barchester Gardens at 176.

41

The British Prisons' share prospectus makes a remarkable series of claims for the future of the company, BritNicks, as it will be known. A message from its chairman, SIR MAX SECURITY beats the drum for British confinement technology: 'We at BritNicks are proud of our country's long tradition in incarceration; Britons have been locking up people for nearly a thousand years. It's an important part of our heritage. And the future has never looked better for the prison industry: an expanding market, international opportunities, a new Criminal Justice Act.

'Never, in the field of human confinement, have so many been banged up for so long by so few. Britain already leads the field and is poised to take a global number one position in penal servitude.'

You're impressed; the plan to turn Essex into a giant penal colony for all European prisoners particularly catches your imagination. You apply for £500 worth of shares. Go to 87.

42

Alas! You have fallen in with one of the most celebrated boozers in Fleet Street and you are about to embark on a rollercoaster of increasingly horrible events as the night progresses. Fortunately the amount of alcohol you consume obliterates them from your braincells the following day; unfortunately the most embarrassing episodes rise unbidden from your memory sporadically over the next week. You never do work out why you wanted to climb through the lavatory window at Langan's Brasserie or steal a bar stool from Zanzibar.

When consciousness cracks its truncheon over your head the following morning, you open your eyes and realize you haven't a clue where you are. As the frenzied percussionist in your head rises to a climax, you stand up and discover you have been sleeping on the floor of a railway carriage. It's not moving. There is no one else aboard. Your watch tells you it's seven o'clock. Through the window you see a distant platform; its sign reads 'Portsmouth'. *You suddenly remember*! C.U. Incourt offered you a shift on the *Grind* diary. Nine o'clock sharp.

You make it to Titanic House, Fleet Street, by ten o'clock, unwashed, unshaven, suit crumpled, feeling like a full ashtray. Incourt looks on you and your lateness with considerable disfavour. An old hand at dissolute behaviour, he has survived the night with no ill effects. A sympathetic diary colleague, ALICE AFORETHOUGHT, slips you a hipflask of whisky; a few swigs and you begin to feel human – well, possibly a higher primate. Incourt offers you two stories to chase up: one about backstabbing at the BBC, the other about a new editor of a glossy mag.

If you want the Beeb, go to [18]. If the glossy, [98].

43

As soon as you turn, you realize that you've found the rightplace. Now you come to think about it, there's the off-licence on the corner that you were told to look out for and halfway down the street is the house itself. It's a classic, if well-worn, London townhouse. Cast-iron railings are broken by steps leading up to a raised front door and by a gate which opens onto a stairway down to the basement. You ring the bell; a bright, female, upper-class voice can dimly be heard crying, 'Oh God, hang on a mo, I'm just coming!' And then the door is opened.

There before you stands a pretty, slightly plump girl. She has blue eyes, English Rose skin and a mass of blonde hair, which is piled up on top of her head, with its dark roots clearly visible. She is wearing a fluffy pink towel and steaming gently.

You introduce yourself and the girl lets you in. She says she's Sophie, shows you where the drinks are kept, says 'Yar', 'Absolutely', 'Chilling', 'Oh Christ' and 'Have you got a Silk Cut?' in no particular order and then heads upstairs to dress.

When Sophie returns she finds a cigarette and a large glass of Frascati and settles down to tell you all about herself, the house and the rest of its inhabitants. Her full name is SOPHIE GODYAH-RALEIGH and she's twenty years old. Her mother, Lady Lymeswold owns the house (Sophie's father died in a shooting accident in 1974; her mother then married his old school chum Nicholas Lymeswold, Tory MP for a Cambridgeshire constituency, recently knighted for seventeen years of voting as the Whips told him). Sophie works for an art dealer in St James, Wildebeest & De Trop, who pay her just over £5,000 p.a. This is naturally not enough for her to live comfortably, despite the rent-free accommodation, and her trust fund (poor Daddy was *so* sensible) tops it up with another £12,000. Her creamy skin and enthusiastic manner also ensure that there is always a large number of men willing to take her to dinner, to country houses or to Gstaad.

Downstairs in the basement lives GEORGE DUSTJACKET, the forty-six-year-old Literary Editor of the new hi-tech serious daily, *The Cursor*, who is estranged from his wife. But the crew who share the rest of the building with Sophie are an altogether younger, livelier lot.

They include JOHNNY STANDFIRST, twenty-four, a university friend of Sophie's brother Peter Godyah-Raleigh (now with his merchant bank in Japan), who is just finishing his two years of provincial training as a journalist on the *Barking Bugle*.

Sophie is wary of Standfirst and describes him as 'Peter's leftie friend', although his politics would have seemed unexceptional in any Conservative Party before Mrs Thatcher became leader. His odd journalistic friends and generally sceptical attitude to authority are, however, the probable cause of Sophie's unease.

Standfirst's ambitions centre around getting a job on Fleet Street and he has eased the ennui of doorstepping Barking housewives rumoured to be carrying on with council workmen by casual shift work on national papers and by running his paper's (rather good) weekly rock review page. He has developed a professional cynicism, but idealistic views of the world emerge quite regularly nevertheless.

SONYA STAGESTRUCK, actress, twenty-four-year-old graduate of Oxford and RADA and another one of Peter's friends, is using the house as a launching pad whilst her career – so she hopes – prepares for blast-off. Her professional work has so far consisted of a TV commercial in which she portrayed a dim-witted shopper in search of the perfect low-fat margarine; a walk-on role as Third Victim in an episode of *Dr Who* (her brains were sucked out by a giant insect from a distant galaxy before the show was five minutes old) and three performances in fringe shows so dire that even *City Limits* gave them only brief, caustic mentions before they sank without trace.

Sonya's hopes currently rest on *Strong Men Wept*, a new comedy radio series starting next month and written by the latest brilliant, irreverent, refreshing (etc, etc) Cambridge Footlights and Oxford University types discovered in reviews at this year's Edinburgh Festival. This, she believes, could be her chance to become the latest in the line of sexy comediennes epitomized by Pamela Stephenson and Emma Thompson. Since Sonya is reasonably talented and unreasonably attractive such beliefs are not entirely without foundation. Even so, hers is a notoriously risky profession, a fact that renders Sonya neurotically insecure about both her ability and her looks.

By comparison, JAMIE POLE-POSITION, twenty-three, has always been a model of assured self-confidence. A colleague of Peter Godyah-Raleigh's in the City, Jamie works as a broker at hotshot Stock Exchange market-makers De Bono Lizard. He has always kept his earnings a closely guarded secret, but Sophie tells you that he has been known to telephone home and dial his salary by mistake. Recently, however, all has been rather less simple for Jamie. An unlucky dip into the Dockland property market coincided with a run on his personal account to leave him a little strapped for cash. The only way he could come up with the £450,000 his creditors required was to sell his chintzy Chelsea townhouse. Since none of the Dockland lofts which he owns has actually been built yet he has been forced to come down to the level of his non-City contemporaries and go back to flat-sharing.

Jamie, however, takes the view that crashes may come and go and bears may be all round, but a chap must maintain standards. So despite his decreased job security and markedly reduced resources he still maintains a lifestyle a sheik would be proud of. He flies on business to New York and Geneva and weekends in Rome, St Moritz or Budapest. On the rare occasions when he has a week to spare from his labours he travels further – Peru, Madagascar, Kenya and . . . Bayreuth. Jamie is a Wagner enthusiast and on his extremely occasional weekends in town the house reverberates to *Die Walküre*, played at 250 watts per channel on his state-of-the-art CD system.

The final inhabitant of the house is Charles Glove-Puppet, an old friend of the Godyah-Raleighs with whom you were at university. Charles works for Concept Consultancy Inc., a major American firm of business analysts who have sent him to Chicago for a year of situational and vocational man-to-man and man–machine interface in the context of a structured, input-heavy, educational environment with employee upgrade potential. In other words, he's on a training course. You've got his room in the meantime.

But what's going to happen to you? The prospect of a new life awaits at 147.

44

SOUND: *Rule Britannia* from Last Night Of The Proms.

TITLE: THE WORLD AS TRAIN SET

Establishing shot of Suffolk cottage, garden gate falls off.

1: F. T. Comment in whites and blazer asleep in front of TV showing cricket.

VOICEOVER (sarcasm *a la* Johnny Rotten): We never lost it! The sun never set!

2: Comment delivers anecdote of ancient retainer of Indian princely family who retains a portrait of Queen Victoria for 'when the British come again'. 'They still have a lot of affection for us you know.'

Cut to:

3: 1850s print of British soldiers tying Indian mutineers to the muzzles of cannon . . .

SOUND: Debussy's *L'apres-midi d'un faune*

TITLE: THE LAVENDER HILL MOB AND THE PURPLE PROSE GANG

Establishing shot of flat interior decorated in rococo with Stanislaus Nuristan in Chinese silk robes.

1: Nuristan reading from own work in a high, fluting voice: 'Beneath the shadow of the mauve hills above Masra the naughty darkness of the East crept on soft gilt sandals through narrow ancient streets, those thoroughfares of a chattering, roughish populace who daily try conclusions with the merchants, an old profession, old even when Alexander, the slimmed-calved Greek boy become potent war-god came *mirabile dictu!* leading his Bactrians . . .

Cut to:

2: Reaction shot of Tim Tryer pretending to throw up . . .

SOUND: *The End* by The Doors

TITLE: AN AMERICAN EMBARRASSED

Establishing shot of a black and white photograph of a young Ingrid Reference smiling up at the man beside her. It is obviously her father, tall, handsome, in the uniform of a US marine colonel.

1: Ingrid Reference today in her Savoy suite in shades, not smiling, twisting her jewellery: 'I think Americans have to come to terms with the fact that they are very rich [quick flash of Krystle Carrington in *Dynasty*] and have responsibilities [quick flash of Donald Duck with his nephews Huey, Dewey and Louie, that they should know more about the world [quick flash of Orson Welles as Citizen Kane], and what those responsibilities are [quick flash of napalm attack on Vietnamese village, cruise missile in flight, Sylvester Stallone wrestling a helicopter to the ground]. I hope my book tries to do that [quick flash of a snowball in hell]' . . .

Go to 97.

45

The symptoms persist in their full agony for three months, then a gentle easing off allows you some mobility. When you can walk around the ward, *The Cursor* wastes no time in having you discharged from the £500 a day hospital. You are still on a generous salary from them of course, but your contract runs out in three months and you are still incapable of doing any kind of work.

You move out of Barchester Gardens because the stairs are such a fag. Your new flat is on the ground floor which helps, but it is in Notting Hill which costs you plenty. Your condition improves. When the contract with *The Cursor* runs out you are obliged to leave. Fortunately you obtain a hard-to-let council flat in a towerblock in the very depths of the East End, Barrow Marshes E18, just before the Central Line tube runs off the edge of the world. It was found by the social worker who kindly visited you. Go to 109.

46

My, aren't we getting grown up? It seems hardly any time since you got off the train at King's Cross, and now here you are about to become a man of property. If you talk your parents into lending you a few thousand for the deposit and mortgage yourself up to the hilt – which, Jamie Pole-Position assures you after you have sought his advice, is by far the best thing to do in the current economic climate – you can just about afford £80,000. In Drabworthy this would buy you most of the town centre, and still leave enough over for a Caribbean holiday, but in London such a figure evokes polite coughs of disbelief from estate agents. You are immediately handed over to the newest, most junior negotiator at every agent's you visit; 'Another first-time buyer for you, I think, Fiona.'

So what do you get for your money? The choice seems to range from an unfitted wardrobe with outside loo in Knightsbridge, through a single-bedroom flat in one of the rougher parts of Notting Hill, to a small two-bed terrace house next door to a Bengali sweatshop in Poplar – real Eastender country. The latter needs a bit of work, but it is a very up-and-coming area and close to your office. The wardrobe is small, OK, but you can't knock Knightsbridge for location.

The flat in Notting Hill is certainly in an area that is drop-dead trendy, close to your old pals in Barchester Gardens and stiff with good restaurants and hip art galleries. But can you afford the flat *and* the lifestyle?

The time has come to make a decision. Remember, the property you buy says a great deal about the person you are. Think of yourself in each of those homes and ask yourself: 'Is this really me?'

The numbers are as follows – you must take one: Knightsbridge, 22; Notting Hill, 140 and Poplar, 149.

47

Charlotte is understandably piqued by your gaffe, but your visible embarrassment goes some way towards soothing her *amour propre*. In any event, it is clear to her that she will learn little of any interest from this party and you appear to be the only man in the room with any conversation beyond pork-belly futures, Porsches and the current state of the grouse moors. So you chat away and manage to recover a little of your credibility. You wax particularly lyrical about a recent trip to Yugoslavia. Evidently Zagreb has a flourishing youth culture and is now, you believe, even trendier than Barcelona. This is music to Charlotte's ears.

At the end of dinner she invites you to lunch in a few days' time. Count yourself lucky and meet her again at 143.

The offices of *The Cursor* are in a converted warehouse in Brixton. The hi-tech newspaper's launch two years previously was a considerable success. Its rigorous toeing of the Tory party line and concern for the prejudices of selfish rich people has brought a comparatively substantial and well-heeled readership, beloved of marketing men. Its proprietor, LORD MAGNUM, has received the statutory life peerage from the government given to rich newspaper owners who know which side their bread is buttered. Next New Year's honours list, Terence Broadsheet will receive the statutory knighthood given to editors who also know this.

Over a lunch in his office of inedible canteen sandwiches and cheap warm white wine, the tiny striped-shirt Broadsheet outlines the future of national newspapers and his in particular. The more

editors you meet, the more you discover that they tend to have particular obsessions. Broadsheet's current bee in his bonnet is bee in his bonnet is finding a disease for the Nineties. He feels that herpes never really got started, and that AIDS, despite a tremendous run in the past few years, has peaked.

'Public interest is tailing off, people don't want to know. The Pope would have to get it before you could sell papers with it again. No, what I'm looking for is next year's disease. And I think I've found it – Yuppie Flu.'

You feel a faint flutter of dread in your intestines as he continues at 111.

49

The Christian Purity League are beginning their march from Conway Hall in Red Lion Square with an address by one of their American founder members and star speakers, the REV. NASAL TONES. You sit at the back, unwilling to be caught up in the squeaky-clean crowd up front. The Rev. revs up, and within a few seconds of his opening address you find yourself strangely moved by his words. It all seems so true! He talks about the emptiness of contemporary life and the wearisome burden of material success and its unending pursuit. This strikes a chord, and you relax for perhaps the first time since you came to the capital. You listen to this man who puts his finger on the problems that have been worrying you. As he talks of the relentlessness of greed, lust and selfishness, you begin to ache with remorse and your shoulders start to heave. In the middle of this crying jag a large, fatherly figure comes up, puts his hand on your shoulder and invites you to come and talk to him about it in a quieter place. It is such a relief to escape from the pressures of ambition. Talking to SIMON SHOULDER, former major in the Marines, you begin to realize the mistakes you have made so far in your life. It comes as no surprise to you that you entirely reform and give up your previous existence. You join the Christian Purity League and work on their social programme. After six months in Liverpool with whores, alcoholics and junkies, you transfer to the League's Beirut medical mission. Your death a year later in a Hizbollah suicide bombing is greeted with expressions of shock and loss by your colleagues in the Lebanon and by the press and politicians at home. During your short Christian career, you became a symbol of a generation's idealism for a Britain lost in soulless materialism. A leader in *The Times* compares you to Mother Theresa. Betcha didn't expect that when you started out in search of FAME AND FORTUNE.

50

Unused to the New York subway system and intimidated by the hellish noise and brutality of both the stations and rolling stock, you take the wrong track and are soon hopelessly lost. You decide to ask directions from the inoffensive little man sitting opposite you. As you cross over to him you reach inside your jacket to get out a map of the system.

How were you to know that this same man had been mugged fourteen times within a month; that he had, in desperation, bought a gun; that he was thirsty for revenge and quick to misinterpret your gesture as that of a potential assailant reaching for a weapon?

The moment you say, 'Excuse me . . .' he pulls out his Magnum and blows you away. You die instantly. As you are lying in the morgue the *New York Post* runs a minor local news story with the heading: 'BRIT BITES BULLET IN SUBWAY SLAYING.' Your killer is found not guilty. ☠

51

You wouldn't really try that old astrology line would you? Where have you been for the last ten years? Do yourself a favour. Turn to 161 and learn a profound truth about female sexuality. It may help you.

52

You stand up against a wall, spread your leg, undo your fly and let rip. God, that feels good. There's a fine spray bouncing back off the wall and against your trousers, and your left shoe is now an island in the stream, but these are minor blemishes. Just as you're finishing you hear a sound in the alley. You twist your head to see a man with a cropped haircut and macho moustache dressed in tight black leather trousers and a white T-shirt. A silver chain girdles his waist.

For all the outward masculinity of his clothing, the man has a mincing walk and his voice, when it comes, is outrageously effete. 'My, my,' he says. 'Just look at that. Isn't *she* a big girl?'

The long-term effects of the booze and the sweet sensation you have just enjoyed have left you in a fine good humour. So you join in the spirit of the occasion. Putting on your best camp voice you call out, 'Cop this ducky. I bet you'd like a slice of *my* tube steak.' With that you wave your willy in his direction, sending a final shower across the alley as you do.

The man's manner changes in an instant. His voice lowers by an octave. 'Right, you little bastard, up against the wall.' Fumbling with your flies you turn back to the wall, hands up against it, legs apart. 'You pervert scum,' says the man. 'Your type really make me sick. You think I like dressing up like a pouf and going out after your kind? You're under arrest.' He doesn't read you your rights. Instead he slams a fist into your kidneys. You collapse face down on the wet, stinking pavement. Through the pain you realize you've been picked up by a 'pretty policeman'. Right now he's radioing his station for assistance.

Then a thought strikes you. The policeman has no idea who you are. If you could make a run for it now and get away before his reinforcements arrived you'd be out of trouble and he'd have no way of tracking you down. And even if you were found again, what could anyone do about it? You haven't done anything wrong. So, do you want to try your luck?

If you want to leg it, sprint away to 146. If you'd rather see what fate has in store for you here, stay still at 108.

53

Well, you've done it.

The exposé appears with the set-up pictures taken in an Islington winebar, Le Truc Futile. The copy accompanying the photographs has little relation to the truth of the two women's touching romance. Rosie Retrial's career suffers no setback, but Cecily is obliged to leave her job at the gazebo charity. Her father, the Bishop of Rockall, 'retires' two months later.

The Ooze of the Globe finally pays you £10,000 for your assistance, but the moral opprobrium which falls on you when it becomes clear you set up a friend and sold her to the papers loses you the esteem of all decent-thinking people. Best lie low for a while and invest your thirty pieces of silver in London's equivalent of 3–2–1. *Tim Tryer, come on down to the property market!* Materialism beckons at 46.

54

Miss Freezeframe has recently been head-hunted by a go-ahead independent TV production company, Nothing Special. She cut her teeth at a radical TV collective, Obscure Opinions, but she has smoothly made the change from revolutionary socialism to capitalism. The expensive playthings of ecstatic hedonism are arriving: Porsche with carphone, country cottage with jacuzzi, Wapping warehouse with toyboy . . . When she sees you in your leathers, Vanessa gets the urge to make a new acquisition. In her forthright way she arranges for your company to send you to make a delivery, and then asks you out to lunch. What do you do?

Vanessa Freezeframe is an attractive, though certainly not beautiful, woman in her mid-thirties, lively and intelligent. If you want to accept her invitation, with any strings which may be attached, go to 171.

If you find yourself horrified at the thought of being the object of this woman's rapacious sexual appetite, go to 150.

55

In your happier moments you toy with the idea of going to South Africa out of sheer mischief, but those are fewer and fewer as weeks go by. You haven't been outside since your discharge; you stay locked in your room at Barchester Gardens. *The Cursor* is still paying you a large salary but your contract runs out in three weeks. Most of the money has gone on ineffective cosmetics and incredibly expensive food deliveries from Fortnum & Mason. Your time is spent watching TV – monochrome, of course. Colour is too painful.

One day the claustrophobia becomes too much and you blow the last of your money on hiring a chauffeur-driven car to take you to Brighton. Wearing gloves, dark glasses, a large deerstalker with the earflaps down and several scarves, a blue-tipped nose emerges from Barchester Gardens and hurriedly gets into a car. It is late autumn. At Brighton the beach is sunny but deserted. You walk for twenty minutes or so, then sit down on the shingle. The sun is warm and you take off your hat and scarves. It's restful looking at the sea . . . the blue sea . . . the blue, blue sea . . .

You fall asleep. Go to 16.

56

You wait anxiously to hear what your colleagues feel about your choice.

Go to 142.

57

You feel as though you are emerging from a long, dark tunnel. Something tells you that you've been in the tunnel for the whole of your life. Certainly you can't imagine where you were when you weren't in the tunnel. A small patch of light gradually increases in size before you. Shapes begin to emerge, as if from a mist. There is a man leaning over you wearing a white coat. He seems like a nice man. Next to him is a woman in a blue dress with a white apron and a funny sort of hat. She seems nice too. Who on earth can they be? Why are you lying down? Where are you and what are you doing there?

You're in St Stephen's Hospital, that's where. It's now Thursday afternoon and you've been out cold since Sunday evening, when you were carried in, covered with blood and suffering from a factured skull. The man leaning over you is a doctor. The woman is a nurse. Neither of these concepts means anything to you at the moment and nor does the question that the man dressed all in dark blue, who is sitting beside your bed, is asking you. The question is, 'What is your name?'

Funnily enough, you haven't the faintest idea. You're suffering from total amnesia. To make matters worse, if you could recall anything you would be aware of the fact that you threw away your wallet, which was gratefully received by your attackers in lieu of the pleasure of smashing your face in (well, the lamp post did that pretty effectively anyway), so there's no documentary evidence of your identity.

At first your parents attribute the fact that they have not heard from you to the general casualness and inefficiency of youth. You'll be busy meeting people, making new friends and trying to find a job. No doubt you'll ring or write as soon as you've got the time.

When a month goes by without a sound from you, worry begins to set in. You hadn't left them the number of Sophie's house and since you'd only described the owners as 'friends of Charles'' your parents have no means of finding out what it might be. Eventually they call the police, but the police are overstretched and can hardly devote their resources to tracking down adults who've failed to call home.

Your father hits upon the idea of calling round all of London's hospitals. But when he calls St Stephens the operator he gets through to is a temp. She doesn't seem to understand what he's trying to say. How could she? She doesn't speak English.

In desperation the family hires a private detective. He follows the path you must have taken from King's Cross. He interviews everyone he can. He badgers the police and visits hospitals in person. Finally, on a cold day in February, with grimy slush sitting on the pavements of London, he leads your parents to your bedside.

Your father says, 'Come on, son, you're going back home again.'

You say, 'Who the hell are you?'

You go back to Drabworthy on the following day. Your memory never recovers, but your father gives you a job packing crates at his factory and the pattern of your life – dull, quiet, but surrounded by kind folk who make allowances for your impaired intelligence – is set. In time you achieve some sort of simple contentment. But your dreams of FAME AND FORTUNE have vanished like whispers on the wind. ☠

58

You feel pleased with yourself setting up as a smack dealer; you're part of Britain's new enterprise culture, a small business established to cater for a burgeoning market. There is no problem finding customers; Reginald Maudling House is filled with clients, you can't go out without tripping over them in the passageways. You give the glue-sniffers free samples in order to encourage them if they manage to nick some money from their parents or mug a terrified OAP. The turnover of the business is soon £10,000 a week, thanks to the considerable customer loyalty, and after two months you've made £50,000. You start wondering if you should expand the business – prospects seem good. Or maybe you should start investing the profit in something more solid like property. Or do you feel you should get out of illegal activity and maybe try your luck back in the straight world?

If you want to move into big time heroin sales, go to 179.

If you want to get out and invest your illgotten gains in bricks and mortar, go to 46.

If you want to go back to Barchester Gardens and try a more conventional career, call Sophie Godyah-Raleigh at 144.

59

The major reason you got the job with Nothing Special is that VANESSA FREEZEFRAME, senior director of the company, has taken a great liking to your body. This is not too desperate: Vanessa is a good-looking, exuberant thirty-four-year-old, wealthy and successful through her work in television. Her penchant for agreeable young men only occasionally becomes sexual harassment, and for the moment you are both working too hard on the next project, a chat show for Lord Magnum's latest addition to his communication empire, Satellite Fantastic. This 24-hour channel will cover all of Europe, beaming down from a 10 million dollar lump of hardware in a stationary orbit above the Atlantic.

SatFan (as its employees call it) is run by the heir presumptive to Lord Magnum's Affair Corp, his nephew, NICHOLAS LEASEBACK. He has been moved from his position as Chief Executive (scheduling) of his uncle's US TV stations to this new post. At your meeting with him at Affair Corp HQ, Power House, his brief to Nothing Special is, 'Revitalize the whole concept of the chat show – we want something new, vital, relevant to today's generation; sharp, slick, unmissable; a sort of *Alas Smith And Jones* meets *Mastermind*; entertaining, witty, sophisticated, but still able to communicate with the common viewer, with human interest; a kind of *That's Life* crossed with *The Young Ones* . . .'

Back at the office, Vanessa explains that what he *really* wants is Wogan but they couldn't afford him.

'You've got to come up with something to compete with the man who put the Tel in television.'

What are you going to do? Find out at 164.

60

'Tim,' says Tony Tot when you meet him, 'I like your style. You're a happening person. You could be perfect for this agency. Take a chair.'

He gestures expansively at one of the objects that litter the gigantic Wapping loft that constitutes his office. Arranged at intervals across the several-acre expanse of bare wooden flooring are the capital of a Roman column, what appears to be a patch of foam-rubber grass about four feet high, a pair of giant red lips and an oversized pencil sharpener. You recline into the grass and the green rubber prongs mould themselves around you to form a seating arrangement. Tot sits about thirty yards away, behind a desk that is artfully shaped to resemble a flock of sheep carrying a stained-glass window on their backs.

Tot gazes thoughtfully out of the giant picture windows overlooking Docklands. The view is obstructed only by the giant fluorescent yellow tubes (whose function is entirely unknown) appended to the building by Richard Rogers when converting a former jute warehouse into BB&T's HQ.

'Let me run a few concepts by you,' he says. 'This is an agency of the future. It's an agency of the world. No one knows this yet, but we intend to buy one of New York's hottest houses. I tell you, Tim, in two years' time *Klondike, Zipper, Yablonski, Barfly, Baffle and Tot* is going to be one of the biggest names in transatlantic advertising.'

You agree that this is certainly probable.

'I want to remind you of some of the moments that have made BB&T what it is today,' Tot continues. He presses a button and an entire wall lights up in a dazzling collage of posters and film stills. You try to turn round to look at it but succeed only in becoming hopelessly entangled in the rubber grass. When, at last, you have freed yourself, you gaze at Tot's greatest hits.

Amongst the pouting models in minimal swimsuits advertising everything from fast cars to fast foods, the dominant images are strictly asexual. There's the famous Monster Raving Loony poster, featuring portraits of Margaret Thatcher, Neil Kinnock and Screaming Lord Sutch. 'They're all crazy,' the slogan reads, 'But only one is honest enough to admit it.' The follow-up features Sutch in front of a line of famous British Prime Ministers. It says, 'Don't be afraid to vote Loony. It's never stopped you before.'

'We've got a tradition here,' says the triumphant Tot. 'And I want you, Tim, to be a part of that tradition.'

Do *you* want to be part of it, though? If so, your concept awaits you at 70. If not, depart for 103.

61

Hey, Tim, so you're a secret medallion-and-chest-wig man? Say, does the word 'feminism' mean anything to you? Still, maybe Lydia likes that caveman stuff. You'll find out on 161.

62

Onwards and upwards you go, just like one of Des Res's skyscrapers. Soon you are the public face of one of Britain's largest property concerns. When two hundred acres of unspoiled greenbelt fields are bought by Des and – thanks to your silver tongue and bottomless slush fund – planning permission is granted for a massive hypermarket and factory complex, yours is the face that local TV viewers see reassuring them on the regional news shows. In your warmest tones you promise your interviewer that your corporation is determined to maintain the character of the countryside. To this end, you reveal, a full ten acres of the site are being retained as 'a park-style leisure environment', complete with a simulated Farmworld animal processing centre where families can come and experience the sights, sounds and smells of a contemporary factory farm; a nine-hole Kra-Z-Golf course where Dad can relax with the topless girl caddies while Mum does the shopping; and a selection of Space Killers and My Little Cockroach fantasy rides for the kiddies.

You devote your whole-hearted efforts to ensuring the brutal desecration of some of the country's prettiest market towns. You charm and smarm as bulldozers and concrete mixers smash hedgerows and obliterate woods and fields. Happily you explain why it is necessary to replace our cities' architectural heritage with faceless shop and office complexes. And you prosper mightily doing it. Des gives you a share option in his company and Kelly-Marie offers a slice of her pert little body. Hubby, it seems, just isn't up to it any more, so you tool down to St George's Hill in your brand-new Porsche and slip it to Kel while the old man's away. Your life is good.

As if to add icing to the cake, your job brings you into increasing contact with the media. Soon you are writing articles opposite the editorial in *The Times* urging the government to abandon all planning controls for the good of Britain's economy. And as franchise renewal time approaches for the commercial TV companies, yours is a name that's heard more and more around the table at programme planning conferences. In the old days a company that wanted to keep hold of its money-printing licence slapped on a few arts and social conscience features to impress the IBA. But nowadays nothing could be more likely to offend the prevailing climate of opinion than too much culture on the box. But an unrepentant, profit-crazed yuppie with an oily manner and a wardrobe full of designer labels – well, it could be perfect for the corporate image, theirs and yours.

A glittering future awaits you. If you want to go straight to it, proceed at once to 93. On the other hand, you've been working awfully hard recently. Why not take a break? You can be spared for a couple of weeks. Enjoy yourself. Fly to the Seychelles, where tropical beaches and crystal seas await you at 136.

63

The project goes well. You buy a word-processor with the advance money and start writing with a vengeance. For the practical details of demolishing buildings without their owners' consent you interview interesting people: steeplejacks, petty criminals, ex-SAS officers, architects, computer hackers.

The manuscript is almost half-finished when you start the section on the Houses of Parliament – Lazlo K has a pathological hatred of Neo-Gothic. Within a few days you begin to feel generally uneasy. Slightly odd occurrences build into a small paranoia: correspondence is inexplicably mislaid – first in the post, then in your files. Previously helpful sources suddenly refuse further assistance with no explanation. You curse British Telecom when your telephone often fails to connect you, and odd noises punctuate your conversations when you do manage to get through.

You laugh at the thought as soon as it enters your mind: am I being watched? But there does always seem to be someone hanging around the corner of the street beside the Art Nouveau antique shop, paying close attention to your visitors.

Puzzled and disturbed, move on to 133.

64

A Kick Up The Arts turns out to be hotter than you can handle. After the first programme there are threats of court cases and the Special Branch are rumoured to be planning a raid. It seems that the item about offering a £1 million cash bounty for anyone who would assassinate the Arts Minister was just a tiny bit over the top.

An old university friend who is now a high-flyer at the Home Office calls to advise you to disassociate yourself as quickly as possible from the show. As a member of the production team you have a much lower profile than you would have done as presenter, so you should be able to bail out without too much damage to your career.

You wangle an interview at Nothing Special, another TV company who are in the market for bright young people with good ideas. After the formal interview you are taken for a drink with a group of directors and senior executives. One of them, a woman, is eyeing you strangely. Have you got the job? Find out at 59.

65

You're obviously ahead of the game here. You win by having two starters, instead of an hors d'oeuvre and main course. Sorrel soup is a Foodie standard, the warm salad a Nouvelle Cuisine essential.

No wine at lunch is a recent import from the US, and now very common among women power-lunchers ('I take responsibility for my body'). It implies a near-religious dedication to their job and an ascetic life-style while still spending large sums of money in restaurants. Power is usually their only vice.

Badoit has beaten Perrier in the designer water stakes – the bubbles are smaller and less exuberant. That's *l'eau* biz.

Move to 112.

66

You collect your £3,000, but when you watch the ITN News that evening you learn that you could have made £749,500 if you had held on until lunchtime. The Roman Catholic Church was involved in a titanic battle with the Rev. Sun Myung Moon's Unification Church for a majority shareholding in the Church of England which pushed the shares up and up.

This makes you realize that playing the market is not the way to fame and fortune for you, and that perhaps it would be easier if you took up the idea of becoming a bike boy after all. Buy your flash machine and kick start your new life at 3.

67

Tim, old sport, you are in *serious* trouble. That was no ordinary bunch of lads you just bumped into, that was the Blue Moon Defective Agency, arguably the world's most psychopathically violent group of football hooligans. They don't carry out their bestial acts of evil because they are the deprived problem-children of an uncaring society. On the contrary, they all have highly paid jobs. They beat people up because they really, really enjoy it. And today, to make matters worse, they are especially looking for trouble. Chelsea, their chosen football team, have just been beaten 4–0 at home in the first televised Sunday afternoon game of the season. The Agency boys were drunk before the match, they maintained their alcohol level at danger point for the full 90 minutes (yes, of course drinking at football matches is illegal, so is maiming people for life – the Agency are experts at both), then after the whistle had blown they hit the bottles and the cans at a significantly increased rate of consumption.

Now they scent blood. Your blood. You're running from them as fast as you can, but you've got a heavy suitcase in one hand and a typewriter in the other. Try as you might you can't seem to prevent them gaining with every stride. What are you going to do? You could drop your bags and make a run for it. It would mean the certain loss of your most treasured worldly possessions, but you might just get away. Or you could stand and fight in the hope that the commotion attracts attention and help arrives. You can run to 168, or make a stand at 11. The choice is yours.

68

When you get to the police station you are booked. Your pleas for a telephone call are ignored and you are dragged off to an interrogation room. Four officers follow you in. Your cuffs are undone and the men form a semi-circle around you.

They start taunting you, calling you a pouf, a bumboy, a nance, a faggot. Then one of them – the one that arrested you – says, 'He waved it at me, but he's so bleeding small I could hardly see it.' Everyone thinks this is the very height of wit and to maintain their high spirits they start jabbing you with punches, not to hurt, but just to wind up your anger even further. You want to lash out. You have been shamed, humiliated, put down.

They know this. The group's leader, a sergeant, steps forward. 'Getting a little hot and bothered, are we? Feel like hitting a policeman, do we? Nah, course we don't, we wouldn't dare. We aren't a man. We've got no balls.' He realizes he's got to you. 'Go on then,' he continues. 'Just you and me. Forget the rest of them. Just you and me. You got the bottle for that?'

Well, have you? If you want to show him that you can fight back, retaliate at 39. If you can still accept what you're getting without striking back, restrain yourself at 174.

69

Nelson Ratings turns out to be entirely genuine. Over dinner at the Savoy Grill he explains that he is in the early stages of putting together a huge Anglo-American documentary TV series on spy scandals. He's hoping to get Oliver North to present it, but he has an immediate need of a researcher-cum-assistant to help put together the proposal document with which he hopes to sell the concept. The job, for which he will pay you $45,000 per annum, plus generous expenses, will involve a great deal of travel on both sides of the Atlantic, but there's no time to waste. He wants an answer immediately and he expects to see you in New York on Friday afternoon.

The flight to Kennedy Airport leaves from 106.

But do you want to leave London yet? You've only just arrived. If you'd rather stay where you are for a while, put down roots at 33.

70

Tot has really got you excited. He outlines a glittering career as a copywriter at BB&T. The package is an exciting one – £22K to start with, plus the use of a company BMW 325i and an account at the Zanzibar. You have, of course, sold out your talent. But these days that's exactly what you're supposed to do, and everyone thinks that it's frightfully clever and much more fun than being a poor but honest writer.

You're teamed up with DARREN WAYNE, a streetwise Cockney art director whose windsurfing gear is kept permanently strapped to the top of his Peugeot 205 GTi. In his lunchbreaks he can be seen practising stunts as he flies up and down the docks outside the office. The two of you are put onto BB&T's latest account, Rownbury's Flavoured Condoms. Immediately you come up with two great lines: 'Birds have always been tasty. Now you can be too' and 'If you're going to use your pencil, don't forget to pack a rubber.' This inspires Darren to create all sorts of whizzbang visual scenarios. Your career is now travelling at Warp Factor 9.

Perhaps it's time you thought of buying a place of your own. Do you want to get into the property market with your new wealth? If so, turn to 46. If not, 13.

71

Tearfully Rose explains that she cannot break off her engagement. The wedding dress has already been ordered and the invitations sent out. And, in any case, abandoning marriage to one of the most handsome and wealthy men in South America in favour of an affair with an obscure young author hardly seems a sensible thing for a girl to do.

She leaves you with that most infuriating of sentiments: 'I hope we can still be friends'. In fact, you hope you get the chance to tear her limb from limb one day. Furiously you call Vanessa Freezeframe's office, only to be told that she has flown to Los Angeles for the weekend.

Luckily for you, however, Miss Freezeframe was not the only one to have admired your performance on *Wogan*. Naomi Nantwich, whom you met at the launch party for your book, is keener than ever to see you. Go to her at 134.

72

When you get to work at Obscure Opinions you find, to your horror, that Vanessa Freezeframe has left the company. Apparently she had received a much better offer to become a director of a light-entertainment production company called Nothing Special. It seems the lure of a magnificent salary, fat expense account and a company Porsche 944S with built-in CD system proved to be too much for her Socialist principles. She, like so many before her, has sold out.

The remaining members of the Obscure Opinions collective (yes, they really are *that* alternative) welcome you to their group and explain the rules. They each take it in turn to do the various jobs required, from directing a programme to sweeping the floor. No line of dialogue or commentary and no frame of film may be either added to or subtracted from a programme without the majority consent of the collective as a whole. The government is to be referred to as 'the so-called Fascist Tory junta' and the Prime Minister as 'That Bastard Thatch.' No jokes are to be made about any ethnic or religious group (including animals) with the exception of 'fat capitalist bastards'. Smoking is banned and so is sexism.

After a week of ideological re-education (as a heterosexual, white male you have a lot to learn), you receive a call from Vanessa. She apologizes for leaving you in the lurch. She offers you another job at Nothing Special. But can you trust her after what she has already done? If so, she awaits at 59. If not, battle on with Obscure Opinions at 104.

73

A few weeks go by. You do the rounds of all the magazine and newspaper features editors, but without much joy. Some of the capital's property-based free magazines give you work, but the reason they employ inexperienced writers like you is that no one else will work for the insulting pittance they pay.

Still, work is work and every little bit helps. Just when you're beginning to feel as though your career is getting underway, the telephone rings at Barchester Gardens. It's Camilla calling for you. She thinks she's pregnant. No matter how wild she may be, she's still a good Catholic and doesn't take the pill. You, naughty boy, did not use a condom.

A few days later she takes a test. She *is* pregnant. Under no circumstances will she have an abortion. Her father insists that the two of you marry – the family name could never be sullied by an illegitimate child. What do you do? A scandal like this could wreck your career.

If you want to be a gentleman and face the music, walk down the aisle at 25. Or perhaps you'd rather leave the country. An old friend from Redbrick is working in New York. Flee to his place at 155.

74

'This won't hurt at all.'

The pain searing down your arm makes you gasp for breath as DR TIM ORR-MORTICE injects you with the Yuppie Flu virus. Then you pass out.

Four days later you almost feel like getting out of your bed at the London Infirmary for Plutocrats. When you try, however, you collapse after a few steps, knocking over the enormous display of pink gladioli 'With Best Wishes from the Editor of *The Cursor*'. The charge for clearing up is entered on the daily bill at £20, just below 'opening window – £10, refilling waterglass – £15'.

Four weeks later you feel just as bad, except that mentally you have sunk into a serious depression. In the short periods when you feel you can relate in any way at all to the everyday world, you express the opinion that it doesn't seem likely that you will ever feel up to writing your signature again, let alone a series of sprightly articles for *The Cursor*. Terence Broadsheet, after taking medical advice and examining how much it is going to cost to keep you in this hospital for another six months, agrees.

However, do you want to be given the pharmaceutical company's treatment? In fact it seems that Broadsheet was not being entirely open with you about its efficacy. It is still in its development stage and some odd rumours have been heard about side-effects.

If you are willing to give the treatment a chance – anything to escape feeling like a wet dishcloth – go to 19.

If you think you probably can't stand any more treatment by Dr Orr-Mortice and would rather place your faith in spontaneous remission, move to 45.

75

The company totter to bed at 1.00 a.m. After a passionate goodnight kiss from Victoria, you stagger upstairs. You've been assigned a large gloomy bedroom on the second floor: the furniture is Georgian, the temperature Arctic. When you turn on the hot tap in the bathroom 50 yards down the corridor there follow two minutes of maniacal banging while the pipes vibrate, and then a thin trickle of cold rust-brown water. Shivering, you brush your teeth and give up on further hygiene. On the walk back to your room you lose all sensation in your fingertips. Panic grips you: you don't want to die of hypothermia in the night. Then unbidden into your inebriated mind comes the thought of Victoria's warm body already snugly in bed. If you want to dismiss this cosy vision from your thoughts and go to the kitchen in search of warmth, go to 12. If you seek human comfort to help you make it through the night, go to 38.

76

The February issue of *Malice* leads on your attack on Loony Lefties and provokes a mixed reaction – not from the editor, who loves it – but from your victims. Two of them, Des Res and Tony Tot, send aggrieved letters, then their lawyers send aggrieved letters and finally aggrieved writs. Lazlo Kunstwerk and Terence Broadsheet, however, both seem to have taken your remarks well and indeed rather appreciate your wit and lack of sycophancy.

Kunstwerk invites you to dinner at 85. Broadsheet wants you to drop by *The Cursor* at 48.

77

By 11.00 a.m. it has risen to £5,000. By midday £10,000. This extraordinary state of affairs has driven the market into a frenzy. It is obvious that there is a major battle between two powerful institutions for control of the Church of England. By 12.30 your nerves can't take the strain any more and you sell for £12,500.

That evening on the television news you learn that the Church of England shares peaked at 2.00 p.m. (you would have made £749,500), and that after one of the most epic struggles seen in the stock market the Rev. Sun Myung Moon's Unification Church finally lost to the superior financial muscle of the Roman Catholic Church. The Pope has flown in to chair the meeting called for tomorrow to elect a new set of directors for the Church of England. Three bishops have already resigned, preferring to take their £100,000 'Golden Amen' without having to go through the rough-house expected at tomorrow's Synod. The Archbishop of Canterbury says he intends staying and will stand by his record. A meeting of curates threatens to operate an overtime ban if there are any compulsory redundancies, and will use mass pickets if there is any attempt to bring in blackleg priests.

You don't care that much either way, since in six weeks you have increased your initial investment 25 times. But what to do with it now?

Now that you're recovered largely from the Yuppie Flu and are comparatively wealthy, you could call up Sophie Godyah-Raleigh and get the room back at Barchester Gardens at £60 a week. Telephone her at 144.

Or you could decide to stay in Reginald Maudling House at £11 a week (paid by the DHSS) and use your money for another money-making deal in the City. Grab the next share prospectus at 88.

78

Rose asks you to lunch at a little Italian restaurant near TV Centre. Over the lasagne and green salad her manner is all competence and professionalism. She wants to know about your book, your previous career, your family background in Drabworthy. Every time you say anything remotely amusing she takes a note of it and asks you to make sure that you can repeat it on demand when you're interviewed tonight.

There's little chance of any progress on the romantic front. But Rose makes encouraging remarks about being around to look after you before the show and even hints at the possibility of dinner afterwards.

But as the afternoon goes by she is not the main thing on your mind. You are most concerned by your forthcoming TV appearance. This is your big chance to make an impact on a national audience. Who knows who might be watching or what opportunities might arise.

The main thing is to have a clearly identifiable image. If you favour playing up the explosive aspect of *Blowing Up Britain*, go for the anarchistic young rebel approach at 26. Alternatively, emphasize the light-hearted wit of it all with merry banter at 148.

79

It's seven o'clock when your cab drops you outside El Vino's Winebar in Fleet Street. You push your way past the crowd of striped-shirt/separate collar, red-faced lawyers by the bar to a table at the far end where you find Johnny Standfirst and a plump, red-haired young man around thirty wearing hornrim spectacles and a tweed suit in screaming bookmaker's check with a watch-chain across the waistcoat. Two empty bottles of Hock stand in front of them. Johnny introduces you to C. U. INCOURT, deputy editor of *The Daily Grind*'s 'diary' (i.e. gossip column).

After another bottle of Hock the conversation has moved from discussion of last week's *Sunday Telegraph* piece suggesting compulsory domestic service for the unemployed through anecdotes about Evelyn Waugh to stories of transvestite peers and members of the Royal Family with trusses. You become aware that Incourt is warming to you and may be about to offer you some work. *The Daily Grind* would be an excellent place to build up contacts, and a springboard to other things. You rack your brains for a juicy story to tell him . . .

You have it! At university you knew a rather beautiful girl called CICELY TOOGOOD, daughter of the reactionary Bishop of Rockall. She was very kind to you after an unhappy love affair and helped you get over it. You lost touch when she left to work for an architectural charity which restores gazebos. Two days ago, however, a friend telephoned to say that Cicely had dumped her current boyfriend and run off with radical feminist barrister ROSIE RETRIAL. You can just see it: BISHOP'S DAUGHTER IN TORRID GAY LOVEPACT!

If you want to be a bastard and shop your friend, turn to 14. If not, 99.

80

Your shifts on the arts pages of *The Cursor* begin with a couple of hours' subbing every afternoon. Your evident enthusiasm and competence impress not only Dustjacket, but the other members of the paper's culture Mafia as well. Soon you are working full days. Then they start giving you occasional reviews – rock concerts, fringe theatre events, touring Bulgarian mime troupes and the like. The ready wit and youthful irreverence of your style even attract the attention of the paper's editor, TERENCE BROADSHEET. He is looking for bright young feature writers to ginger up *The Cursor*'s stodgy pages. He summons you to lunch.

You're definitely feeling that things are looking up when you go to meet Broadsheet at 48.

81

Terry takes you to The Wok of Ages, London's newest designer Chinese restaurant. He leads you to a table where two very thin, very pale young men are almost lost under their respective heaps of matted dreadlocks. 'Tim, meet WINSTON and DELROY. They bad.'

Winston and Delroy are, did you but know, the Hon. PERCIVAL PACKET and his elder brother ROLLO, the 14th Viscount Silverfoil. Both have rowed and played racquets for Eton and spent three years in the Coldstream Guards before leaving for a life of trust-funded nightclubbing. They not bad. They fake.

'Like, aah, hi,' drawls Winston/Percival.

'Chillin',' agrees Delroy/Rollo.

Over a long meal and many lagers, it emerges that Terry and his two pals are thinking of opening a nightclub of their own. The trouble is, Terry's too young to drink, let alone apply for a licence. Now, the two pseudo-Rastas are rich enough to fund the venture and well-connected enough to ensure the attendance of London's finest debutantes and their delights, plus a whole bundle of authentic street cred types. But they can't quite come to grips with the idea of doing any actual work. So would you like to be the club's manager? It would be a lot of fun and they'd give you a 25% share in what could be a lucrative operation. But can you face dealing with these idiots? If not, call it a night and wander home via 127. If you are prepared to take a major career risk, gamble your future on 157.

82

Nelson Ratings' invitation sounds pretty interesting and a quick glance around the room tells you that Lydia Eustace is leaving, so you've missed your chance there. But was there something a little disturbing in Nelson's eagerness to dine with you? If you suspect his motives, there's still just time to get to Sophie's dinner at Hamish Urquhart's. He sounds pretty laid-back and wouldn't mind if you turned up to see him at 138.

On the other hand, Nelson Ratings could give you a great job in international television with all the glamour and wealth that that implies. Take a chance with his proclivities at 69.

83

It takes several weeks to put together your story, during which time you live off DHSS handouts and scrounge rooms for the night off members of the Obscure Opinions production team. When the programme finally comes out it is packed with damning evidence about the British judicial system. But rather than looking like a martyr, you just come over as a whingeing, grubby, social outcast. You have begged all your old friends to watch the programme in the hope of ingratiating your way back into your old life. In fact it serves merely to confirm them in the view that they should have nothing to do with you.

In the end you admit defeat. You go back to Drabworthy and abandon all hope of a glittering career in the London high life. Your parents are deeply ashamed, both of the original court case and of the embarrassment caused to them by having their son on the telly in such circumstances. But they eventually agree to take you in.

Embittered by the whole process, you join an extremist group of Left-wing activists. A job is arranged for you in the police monitoring group of a local far-left council. There you proceed to take every opportunity to frustrate and impede police activities. It is some sort of revenge, but hardly the FAME AND FORTUNE of which you dreamed when you set off from Drabworthy. ☠

84

Des Res offers you a whopping £30K plus a car of your choice up to £12K, plus low-cost financing to help you buy a Res-made residence. In return you are to become his spokesperson, telling the world about the wonders of Des's developing.

If you take the job you will gain lots of money, but lose lots of friends. It may be unfair, but no one really likes a property developer. If you feel that the money is worth the disapproval, put on your best suit and a plausible manner and smooth-talk over to 175.

But perhaps you would prefer something a little closer to your original creative aims. If so, say no to Des and see what Tony Tot has to say about the advertising industry. He's waiting for you still at 60.

85

It takes some time to find Lazlo Kunstwerk's flat. He lives in a warehouse in Bermondsey: 4 Guano Buildings, Opium Wharf SE1. Finally you reach it up a cobbled alley so badly lit you keep stumbling over the BMWs parked on the pavement. A video entryphone security system photographs you, X-rays you and demands your credit card before allowing you access.

Lazlo K., in a grey designer boilersuit, greets you at his door on the fourth floor. You can't help noticing he is in a wheelchair. Remorse grips your heart as you remember your article and imagine that Kunstwerk read it as he recovered in hospital after some horrible accident. However, you then notice that behind him everyone else is moving around in wheelchairs across the vast polished metal floor. Kunstwerk offers you one and explains that they are a Twenties' tubular steel design by Gropius – he found the last six originals in Hamburg. Apparently it's one of the great design icons of the 20th century. There are rather a lot of those in this huge flat – nothing seems to be given houseroom unless it is black, made in stainless steel or drawn up by the Bauhaus Group in 1928.

The far wall has four bicycles mounted on it. Kunstwerk explains: three late works by the Finnish craftsman VELO MUDGAARD, and a Belgian masterpiece by an anonymous artist known only as The Master of the Zinc Wingnut. He shows you what seems like a dustbin filled with breezeblocks. 'My sound system,' he informs you and inserts a compact disc. The new Philip Glass opera based on the life of Walt Disney is heard from loudspeakers disguised as 1950s refrigerators.

'But come and meet the others,' says Lazlo.

You grab a tyre in each hand and move to 4.

Inside the noise is deafening. You are greeted by Lazlo who has been here at least half an hour, and is obviously on the outside of at least half a dozen champagne cocktails. After the press photographers have recorded the co-authors (Lazlo is rather unsteady and wraps an arm around your neck) you plunge into the crowd. You prise yourself away from insistent diary writer PETER PENWALLET, whose 'Autolycus' column has long been one of your least favourite sections of *The Sunday Sentinel*.

Among the glamorous throng of celebs (and less glam collection of journalists and freeloaders) are two people eager to speak to you. They are ROSE SWIFTLY, researcher for *Wogan*, and NAOMI NANTWICH, producer of *A Kick Up The Arts*, a new

radical culture slot on Channel 4, which will begin its first series in a month's time. Both are keen to size you up for their shows.

Rose has already taken you for a drink at Zanzibar and you were immediately fascinated by her wide-apart grey-green eyes. At the party here tonight she looks irresistible in her black and white houndstooth suit. She smiles at you across the hall and waves, shaking her ash-blond hair. A spasm of romantic lust makes you wince.

Naomi you have only spoken to on the phone, and she now introduces herself at the party. She has everything a man could want: large biceps, ginger moustache, firm handshake . . . In conversation you realize that what she is offering on her programme could be more than just publicity, it might lead greater things. You also realize that these two TV opportunities are mutually exclusive. Do you continue talking to Naomi Nantwich? If so, go to 134. If you would rather tell her you're not interested and go try your personal and professional luck with Ms Swiftly, go to 7.

87

The BritNicks issue is oversubscribed three times but in the ballot you emerge with all the shares you applied for. When the market opens you sell them at a premium of 100%. Impressed by this form of easy money you invest your money in the next privatization give-away offer from the Government, the Church of England.

The disestablishment of the Church provides an opportunity for unique investment potential, you realize, not least in the large amount of prime site property in central locations ripe for development throughout the country. You put your £1,000 in the oversubscribed issue and again hit the jackpot by receiving all your shares in the ballot (your Sunday School certificates and record of C of E baptism and confirmation also weighted the draw in your favour). When the market opens in the shares, you find that your investment is worth £3,000.

Do you sell your holding now, or wait to see what the market will do?

If you want to sell, go to 66.
If you want to take a chance and hold on, go to 77.

88

You realize that stagging privatized companies is all right, but that if you really want to make serious money you need to go into futures. A future is merely the right to buy or sell a share, commodity or currency at a fixed price at a certain date in the future. If gold is currently at $350 an ounce and you think it is going to rise to $380 in three months, you can buy a future to buy at say, $360. You don't have to pay all the money up front, you pay a percentage, say 10%. Thus you can buy ten times as many contracts and thus make ten times the profit if gold rises. If it doesn't, you're wiped out. Futures are one of the reasons that there are so many Porsches in the City, and why there are so many future traders in jail – it's much better to play this game with other people's money.

You decide to go for currency. The sterling/exchange is currently $1.80. You gather from the press that it might rise to $1.90 in three months. Smart City gossip, however, suggests that it will fall to $1.700. Do you buy futures at $1.85 or $1.75? If the first, go to 113. If the second, 153.

89

Congratulations! You have chosen the median fashionable menu of the late 1980s. *Gravad Lax* has been batting strong since the late Seventies, ousting smoked salmon, the expense-account businessman's fave hors d'oeuvre. It's still holding its own against the strong challenge of Japanese raw fish.

Lotte (Monkfish) was largely unknown to restaurant diners until ten or so years ago. Now it stands near the top of the fish league with swordfish steaks and salmon.

California wines are now mainstream trendy. You might have trumped it with a New Zealand Sauvignon.

Move to 112.

90

Your digital alarm wakes you at seven o'clock. After a quick shower you dress and leave Barchester Gardens. At South Ken tube-station you buy all that morning's newspapers. Starting with the tabloids, you read them all in the Greasy Spoon Cafe over egg, Spam, beans and chips washed down with pints of lurid orange tea. By 8.30 you are at Titanic House, Fleet Street, home of *The Daily Grind*. By dint of patience with the surly porters and perseverance with the maze of corridors, it only takes you half an hour to reach the diary desk – the far corner of the vast, low-ceilinged newsroom. There are no windows. The total depressing effect is of a re-creation of the Somme using banks of desks, typewriters, telephones and enormous quantities of wastepaper. One person only is visible; from the noise he seems to be shouting down the phone to Ulan Bator (he is in fact shouting at a reporter in Hayes, Essex).

A telephone rings – you find it under a pile of yesterday's *Grinds*. It's a message for C. U. Incourt who arrives as you are typing it out on a typewriter so huge and ancient you expect it to have a gear stick. He's in charge while the diary editor, the celebrated SIMON SPORUS is recuperating from his facelift on Mauritius. Your colleagues, ALICE AFORETHOUGHT and KENNETH EAGER, appear and you all settle down to the list of the day. Your homework over breakfast pays off; C.U. is impressed with your grasp of this morning's press.

He offers you two stories: one of backstabbing at the BBC, the other about a glossy magazine. If you want to take the Beeb, go to 18. If the glossy, 98.

91

Hey, you're pretty kinky, aren't you? Can't wait to get into those old rubber pyjamas and get down to the really heavy stuff no doubt. Well, you'll just have to wait a little longer. Turn to 161 and you'll find out why.

92

You've always secretly fancied yourself as a bit of a rock'n'roller. You may look like a typical bourgeois careerist, but underneath that imitation Italian designer suit from Next, there beats a heart of denim and leather. So much so, indeed, that you can play the whole of *Brothers In Arms* on your Slazenger racket.

So Charlotte's proposal of a feature on upper-class rockers goes down like a shot. It is, of course, one of the enduring fantasies of young upper-class ravers and the magazines that cater for them that all rock stars are concealing a public school past. We all know about Genesis and Charterhouse, but did you realize that at least three of the Rolling Stones are Old Harrovians and that David Bowie (who really *is* a thin white Duke) was once in Pop at Eton? No? Well then, there you go.

The problem for would-be aristo rockers is that the huge quantities of money, high-octane nasal pick-me-ups and sexually compliant young women that are the inducement to naturally indolent musicians to get out of bed in the morning (or at least by tea-time) are freely available to them anyway. Why bother to turn up at video shoots, recording sessions, concerts and tedious meetings with agents when you are – in every sense of the word – loaded already. It's the hunger factor, or lack of it, that prevents today's peerage making a really serious assault on the charts.

This is your theory, anyway. And, like any good journalist, you've got your conclusions thoroughly formulated well before they have time to become confused by the presence of research. Even so, you'll need a quote or two. On yer bike, Tim – your subjects await you at 34.

93

Money, telly, Kelly-Marie – surely this is the FAME AND FORTUNE of which you dreamed. You are on the threshold of spectacular success. But you go no further for you, Tim Tryer, are the victim of a terrible property crash. No, the *price* of property doesn't crash. This is all too literal – a thirty-five storey Sixties block that Des is about to demolish to make way for a mock-Georgian semiconductor plant mysteriously collapses with you inside it. You were preparing the site for a visit by the Prince of Wales when the disaster happened and the royal connection ensures maximum publicity. The tabloids stretch the truth a mite and report 'PRINCE IN TOWER OF DEATH DRAMA PROBE' whilst the *Wapping Weekend* assigns forty-three Foresight reporters to discover 'The concrete evidence of shoddy building' and answer the question, 'Could it happen again?' Their four-page report is accompanied by a vast and incomprehensible illustration showing how, they claim, micro-organisms ate into the imported Polish concrete from which the building was constructed. They say that two hundred similar blocks are in imminent danger of collapse. That may well be true, but they have missed the point. The answer to the question, 'Could it happen again?' is actually, 'Yes, but only if someone else is daft enough to try to sleep with Des Res's wife when he thinks the boss isn't looking.' ☠

94

You make your little joke about the party game to Charlotte Van Dryver and she manages a slight smile, which is not entirely encouraging but not a total defeat either. So you start on general conversation – who you are, what you're doing in London, your ambitions and so on. Charlotte reveals that she is not usually the kind of woman to attend such an intellectually undemanding party, but she happens to be researching current trends in dinner-party manners for her magazine *Malice*, the incredibly bitchy, impossibly stylish society bible.

You remember an item about *Malice* from the *Guardian* media page and try to display your knowledge: 'Haven't you got some appalling brand-new editor that no one's ever heard of?'

'Yes,' replies Charlotte.' That's me.'

Oh Lord, Tim, you've really put your foot in it this time. If you think you can rescue the situation with such an important contact as Charlotte, soldier on at 47. If not, Camilla's still there at 36.

95

Do us a favour. You shouldn't be driving. Just consider what you've had to drink so far tonight. There were three, no four white wines at the gallery opening. At least a bottle's worth of red and white wine at the restaurant. Half a bottle of champagne when you toasted Johnny and Sonya. Frankly it was a miracle you made it to Soho in one piece and with your licence intact.

Then, between twelve-thirty and three you moved on to champagne cocktails and straight brandies – nine or ten glasses' worth at the very least. You can barely find your way to the Gents, let alone the car park.

When you finally find your motor it takes you several minutes to fit the key in the lock. Then you get in on the passenger's side and cannot for the life of you work out why the car isn't moving. Actually, you think it *is* moving, but that's just your head spinning around and around in ever increasing circles.

Finally you start the car and it lurches out into the street. As you turn into the wrong lane in Shaftesbury Avenue (utterly ignoring the motorcyclist who came off his bike as he desperately attempted to avoid you) you see Johnny and Sonya waiting for a cab. You wave happily at them. With both hands. The car goes out of control, hurtling off the road, across the pavement and smashing into the foyer of the Apollo Theatre.

En route it also pulverizes Sonya. She is paralysed from the waist down. When your case comes up in court Johnny gives an exact account of the evening, including the number of drinks you downed. The sight of the beautiful Sonya, now a tragic cripple, moves the jury to tears and the press to a frenzy of hateful headlines. 'THE YUPPIE MANIAC WHO SMASHED SEXY SONYA' is one of the mildest. It is generally agreed that you should be flung into jail and the key should be thrown away. You are the very epitome of the evils of drunken driving.

In the end the judge sentences you to seven years and bans you from driving for life. He also awards Sonya £750,000 damages in respect of her lost career. Go to jail at 119. Consider yourself lucky not to be staying there for life.

96

With scrupulous attention to what the authors were trying to say, you produce and edit an eight-minute compendium of anecdotes and illuminating remarks on the nature of travel writing in the late Eighties. You submit what you feel to be a fine piece of work to Naomi Nantwich and wait at home for her to call you with her delight and applause.

Three days later a cheque arrives in the post paying your expenses plus a kill fee for the report. On the Brute Features compliments slip Naomi Nantwich brusquely informs you that your work will not be screened since it does not have a 'sufficiently radical perspective' and that perhaps the South Bank Show might be a better outlet for your rather conventional approach to the arts. This does not disconcert you for more than a moment, they all seemed a collection of berks at Brute Features anyway. Since making money on *Blowing Up Britain* you've been beginning to feel that that the incestuous and bitchy atmosphere of the media is too claustrophobic for your talents and that Eighties' Britain has more to offer a bright boy like you if you went into property. With your fat cheques from Hale & Hearty and *The Cursor*'s serialization banked, you let your fingers do the walking through the Yellow Pages' Estate Agents section.

Go to 46.

97

You can tell things are going well. At Brute Features the secretaries all know your name and smile when you come in: 'Hi Tim!'

Naomi Nantwich and her chums loved your report ('such a radical perspective on this late humanist class-defined nostalgia binge') and want you to do more – perhaps a regular slot on *A Kick Up The Arts* (now two weeks away from its first transmission) maybe called *Feet of Clay*? They offer you a regular job as presenter, or as a commissioning editor.

Which do you prefer?

Presenter? Grab your Paul Smith suit and go to 32.

Editor? Buy more pages for your Filofax and go to 64.

98

C.U. briefs you on the story: the fashionable glossy monthly *Malice* has recently appointed a new editor, CHARLOTTE VAN DRYVER. Curious rumours abound concerning her contract – the salary is enormous, *bien sûr*, pretty certainly £70,000 – but there are supposed to be certain conditions: everyone over thirty fired from the mag; no one under 5 feet 4 inches to be hired; no member of staff to wear Chanel (she wears nothing else); no oranges allowed in the office; the words 'clipboard', 'several', 'useful', 'gusset', 'too', and 'bassoon' all banned from articles.

You decide to try the most direct approach and call her directly. You get through to her assistant who doubts she will speak to you. After holding the call for five minutes and being obliged to listen to a Muzak tape of Bulgarian *a cappella* girls' choirs (another Van Dryver innovation, no doubt) her assistant tells you that if you turn up in person at *Malice* in twelve minutes you can speak to Miss Van Dryver for three.

Perspiring heavily you arrive at her office with seconds to spare. You are shown into her office immediately. She is apostrophizing her features editor, BABETTE DRILLER, saying she cannot *bear* to run another article on Barcelona and its nightclubs. 'There *must* be somewhere else!'

'Zagreb,' you hear yourself saying.

Both women turn. You describe your stay in the Yugoslav city two months ago and the extraordinary evenings you spent drinking plum brandy with disaffected Slav youths, who have a subculture called Balkan Sobranie. Van Dryver muses, 'Slav to love, Yugoslav – I go wild, From Cradle to Zagreb . . . yes, there's something there.'

You get your diary story and, what's more, an invitation to lunch at 143.

99

It's eight o'clock; the fourth bottle of Hock is finished and El Vino's is closing. Incourt asks if you are looking for work, and then offers you a shift on *The Daily Grind* diary tomorrow. You accept gratefully, pleased at Incourt's obvious encouragement. He then suggests that the three of you should carry on drinking somewhere else. Johnny is keen and so are you, but you already feel slightly drunk.

If you give in to their insistent invitations, go to 42. If you would rather go home to bed, catch the 22 bus at 90.

100

BBC Television Centre at White City lacks the historic presence of Broadcasting House, but you are excited by the prospect of working for this great organization. It takes you an age to find Peter Punchline's office in its endless corridors, and then it takes his secretary an age to find him.

He arrives, apologizes and begins to outline some ideas he's got in the pipeline. After twenty minutes of background, he quite suddenly asks you if you would like to be his assistant on his biggest project, *The History of Sex*, a 20-part series, to be produced in collaboration with a US company.

Do you take the job and join the Beeb? Or would you rather retain your freelance freedom?

If you want to come in from the cold, go to 169. If not, 123.

101

The vicars' and tarts' riot goes splendidly. Police reinforcements have to be brought in and tabloid photographers have a field day taking snaps of harassed policemen preventing Danny La Rue-lookalikes throttling Cliff Richard clones. Vanessa gets some good material in the can for her documentary on the social healthiness of public violence, provisionally entitled *The F-Plan Riot*. She invites you and Johnny for a drink and you are delighted to find that her radical opinions do not prevent her belonging to a small exclusive club off The Strand where you spend the rest of the afternoon drinking chilled Stolichnya.

Vanessa claims to be taken by your thorough familiarity with right-on left-wing philosophy, almost all of which you picked up listening to your university dons' reminiscences about college life

in the days when students would rather go to demos than job interviews. But your ideological commitment is, to say the least, sketchy and, as the evening wears on, Vanessa seems to be devoting more and more of her time to the process of mentally undressing you (undertaken, she claims, with the sole intention of letting you know how women feel when men sexually harass them). So you begin to wonder whether it's your mind she's really after. In any case, by the time the bottom of the second bottle is reached she has made you a momentous promise. Turn up at Obscure Opinions on Monday week and she will give you a job there. At last – a break into television. It awaits you at 72.

102

You keep on walking down the road, past the group of men that is now spread out across the pavement. As you make your way by them they force you to push your way through with your shoulders. You notice a heavy, repellent smell of alcohol. You notice, too, a heavy cloud of anger that hovers around them. Now that you're closer you see that their clothes, though clearly expensive, are dirty, scuffed and even torn. Is that blood that's been splashed down one of the shirts? There's no time to take a second look. You don't want to stick around a moment longer than you have to. Get out of here. Turn the corner and hightail it to 67.

103

You get back to Barchester Gardens to find Sophie Godyah-Raleigh, Johnny Standfirst and Sonya Stagestruck contemplating the menus for the local Chinese, Indian and Italian takeaways and leafing through the list of films available from their local video hire shop. Tonight is evidently going to be spent at home. But tomorrow is Friday and a choice of weekends soon presents itself.

Johnny is staying in town. He's heard down the grapevine that owing to an administrative cock-up the Christian Purity League and the Amalgamated Union of British Prostitutes, Streetwalkers, Rent-Boys and Associated Trades will both be marching on Trafalgar Square at exactly the same time on Saturday afternoon. The resulting collision could make great copy, so he suggests you come along to lend a hand. One of you can cover the vicars and the other the tarts and you'll file a joint story to whichever Sunday paper pays the most.

The girls, however, are off to the country for the weekend. Sophie's parents are away and have said she can have the use of their large house outside Cambridge. Do come along too, they say, it'll be lots of fun. All sorts of people are turning up.

Johnny is staying at 172. The girls are off to 124.

104

Your first major story is to be a glowing report on the fantastic success of the Sandinista government in Nicaragua, concentrating on the happiness of the liberated proletariat, the efficiency of the collective economy and the close fraternal and sororial ties between Managua and some of London's more right-on boroughs. So you go off to Central America and put the word about that you're looking for evidence of the triumph of the revolution.

The trouble is that there are large numbers of people in Nicaragua, not to mention Washington DC, who have a very strong vested interest in ensuring that the revolution is anything but triumphant. In fact, they have a powerful desire to see it fail at the first possible opportunity. The last thing that they want to see is a programme on Gringo television praising their sworn enemies. So you can hardly blame them for wanting to see you removed. Permanently.

One day your hired jeep blows up with you inside it. You are killed instantly. If it makes it any better, you may care to know that you become a revolutionary hero, right up there on a million rebellious bedroom walls with Che Guevara. The Obscure Opinions documentary is entitled *The Martyrdom of Timothy Tryer*. And if that isn't enough celebrity for you, try this ... Fawn Hall shredded your death warrant. ☠

105

Dawn arives at 6.00 a.m., its first light greying the windows of the kitchen. You wake and try to get back to sleep, but the killing hangover drilling your temples soon puts paid to that idea. Your mouth is dry and foul and you decide some water and serious painkillers are in order if you are to participate properly in this weekend. As you grope your way through the half-light to the door you slip on something wet and fall over an unpleasant soft pile on the floor. You get up and switch on the light. To your horror a grimacing Labby lies slumped, head back, half beneath the kitchen table. A pool of blood beginning at Labby's head covers a large part of the floor which is liberally sprinkled with broken glass. You sit down heavily as the full enormity of your crime floods your soul. Your hangover has disappeared, and been replaced by an awful sense of doom.

You, while a guest of your landlady Sophie Godyah-Raleigh, have returned her hospitality by drunkenly bludgeoning her beloved sixteen-year-old Labrador to death with a whisky bottle. Go to 128.

106

New York bowls you over. Ratings has installed you in a suite at the Meridien Hotel, overlooking Central Park, with a view that stretches all the way to Harlem. In the evenings, after another day of fascinating work, you watch the dusk fall in tones of purple and misty grey over the soothing green of the park while the lights twinkle on all down Fifth Avenue. Then you change for dinner and head out for yet another night on the town.

One day you have to head out to Brooklyn to interview a former CIA agent. The traffic's terrible, so you decide it would be quicker to take the subway. The station's at 50.

107

'Oh God, Oh God, don't stop, . . . aah, aah, ohmigod that's wonderful . . . oh, please, please, please, just, just there yes, that's . . . oooohhhhhh . . .'

You stud. You really turned it on tonight. And Rose turned out to be a wildcat. Beneath her severely sexy executive houndstooth suit her lithe body was clad in an array of flimsy French underwear put together with a fetishistic artfulness Helmut Newton could not have bettered.

By five in the morning you are lying in a haze of divine exhaustion, sexually satiated, physically drained, incapable of further action. As Rose begins to flick her tongue encouragingly up your inner thigh you realize that you are being called upon to get back to work. This will almost certainly kill you. Change the subject.

'When do you think you'll have any news about the show, darling?' you inquire.

'I won't,' Rose replies.

You are stunned. And it gets worse. Rose reveals that she could not possibly recommend you for the show. Not when you're having an affair. It would be unprofessional.

This is terrible. Midway through last night you had the chance of two TV appearances. Now you have none. There's only one thing to do. Go home, grab some rest and then call Naomi Nantwich. Just keep your wits about you, pray that she wasn't offended by your sudden disappearance with Rose last night, and see if you can fix something with her. Turn to 134 and hope for the best.

108

You sit in the alley, stunned at what has happened. There must be some mistake. You try to be conciliatory. 'I'm very sorry, officer, but there seems to have been some sort of misunderstanding. I didn't mean any harm. It was all a bit of a joke, had a bit too much to drink, I'll admit, but nothing serious.'

He is not impressed. 'Nothing serious? How about gross indecency and assaulting a police officer for starters? I'm going to see you put away, you filthy scumbag.'

Now panic grips you. 'You can't do that. I haven't done anything wrong. If this goes any further I'll make sure that every newspaper in the land gets to hear of it. You can't just arrest me. This is worse than South Africa.'

Before he can answer, the sound of a wailing police siren fills the air. The alley is flooded with whirling blue light as a van pulls up at the end. Four more policemen jump out, pick you up and hurl you into the back of the van. It starts up again and races off into the night, speeding you to your destination at 68.

109

Only after you move in do you realize why all the flats in the block are hard-to-let. Reginald Maudling House is quite celebrated in its way. Whenever TV documentaries run stories on inner-city decay, they always mention this building as, statistically, the most multi-deprived area in Southern England. It is an investigative journalist's paradise: drug addiction, racial attacks, single parent families, prostitution, protection rackets, arson, mugging, Chinese triads, urban terrorists, animal liberationists . . . whichever problem you want they are all conveniently packaged in Maudling House.

You only get mugged every other time you go out, which isn't often since your physical condition is still quite frail. You pick your way through the glue-sniffers on the stairs (the lifts haven't worked since 1986), out through the spray-painted entrance (rather like a late Jackson Pollock), across the windy derelict expanse of weeds and breeze blocks to the heavily barricaded Bangladeshi grocer at the corner. Returning with your baked beans, you settle down to your television (your box habit is up to ten hours a day). *Afternoon Plus*, *The Young Doctors*, *Isaura the Slave Girl*, *Jackanory* and on and on and on. You'll watch anything. Intermittently you take swigs from a bottle of sweet British sherry. Oblivion comes with the testcard.

Was it for this the clay grew tall? What is happening? Get a grip on yourself, Tim. FAME AND FORTUNE are still possible if you can snap out of this cycle of depression and ill-health. Go to 20.

110

After a day's satisfying and profitable work you return to your immaculate flat. It is a typical Notting Hill evening – the high-class atmosphere of Holland Park blending with the relaxed bohemia of Portobello and Ladbroke Grove to produce a unique mix of chic and street.

You decide to check out one of the great new galleries that have opened up in the area. Gallery 25 are having an opening night party, full of pretty girls. And the wine is free and plentiful.

By a happy stroke of good fortune you bump into your old friends from Barchester Gardens, Sonya Stagestruck and Johnny Standfirst. You go out to dinner together at a local restaurant and after a drink or two Johnny confesses that he's been hiding something from you. That afternoon he proposed to Sonya. And she accepted.

It seems that after eighteen months of living in the same house as friends they became lovers. Now they are to be man and wife. Well, this is a piece of information that deserves a *serious* celebration. 'Let's make a night of it,' you declare. 'It's all on me!'

Off you head to Soho and a riotous night of fun. You feel young and happy and on top of the world. By three in the morning you also feel knackered. So you wish your friends a fond farewell and begin to make your way home. If you want to drive back, motor off to 95. If you think you'd be better off trusting to public transport, try 127.

111

'It's just the thing for our readers,' explains Broadsheet. 'They're young, well-off, and terrified of death and age. They have the horrors imagining what it must be like to be unable to ski, eat *boeuf en croute*, drink magnums of Chateau Petrus or screw their secretaries. But they're fascinated as well.

'I want to run a series – My Story by a young, successful yuppie, how it happened to me. I want you to write it.'

'But I don't have Yuppie Flu.'

'We'll give it to you.'

'*I don't want it!*'

'Look, Tim, relax. The symptoms are just like a bad cold with a touch of Alzheimer's. It's non-fatal. And more importantly, Pill Corp, the drug manufacturers, have already produced a successful treatment. However they obviously don't want to announce it until people know about the disease – there are no bucks in curing something no one's ever heard of. And that's where you come in.'

'I still think it sounds terrible.'

'We'll pay you £30,000 and make you senior feature writer. It'll only be for three months and then you can take the cure. What do you say?'

Well, what do you say?

If you fancy a job, lots of money and a dribbly nose for a bit, go to 74.

If you would rather not run up a serious laundry bill in handkerchiefs, go to 5.

112

The meal is completed. The dining-room is beginning to empty. Piers Halfcut left early through the window, after explaining to Bronwen Heilbron about a small oversight he made in her most recent US book contract. It seemed a preferable alternative to being punctured with a marrow spoon.

The glossy posse follow out Sydney Darwin and a giggling Belinda Promo who are going for coffee to his *garconniére* around the corner in Golden Square. His hand is prominently placed on her left buttock.

Over the *espressos*, Charlotte Van Dryver comes to the point of this meeting. She's been confirmed in her opinion of you as a sharp observer of fashionable life. Now she wants to commission an article from you for *Malice*. Two suggestions are made: a piece on some young upper-class types who have formed a band called The Idle Rich, or a survey of successful London left-handers (working title: *Dangerous Lefties*).

If you fancy the aristo rockers, Van Dryver will brief you at 92.

If you'd rather investigate the sinister idea, go to 177.

113

In fact the dollar only goes to $1.88 but you still manage to make around £80,000. At this point you feel your luck has been running too long for it to continue and you prefer to invest some of your money in that cast-iron investment of contemporary London – property. Grab an estate agent's list at 46.

114

Whether you went with Mounting and Joist or O'Mallet, Mel, Del and Tel, it makes no difference. Any conversion of any old building always reveals horrors the survey missed and can be absolutely relied upon to cost twice as much and take three times as long as you ever, in your worst nightmares, believed possible.

The total bill runs to £35,000, and there's worse to come. Your concentration on your house has meant that your work has suffered. It gets worse. Who the hell wants to trek out to Poplar every time they want to see you? You have to spend all your time driving in and out of the West End, so any gains you may have made by being close to your work have been more than cancelled out by being away from the rest of your life. There's only one conceivable bonus – some of your more Left-wing acquaintances are impressed by your migration to such a proletarian neighbourhood. Only the anarchists amongst your neighbours don't feel quite the same way as your friends. They resent your presence and the way in which people like you with their poncey foreign cars (yours is, incidentally, long gone) are taking over their area. That's why they've just sprayed 'Fuck off yupie skumbag' all over the brand-new white paint on the walls of your house.

You've spent far too much; you hate the area; you've lost any work you had because you're always late; you've got to sell your house and move back into Barchester Gardens. Proceed to 103, much the worse for wear.

115

Pausing only briefly to pick up a glass of champagne from one of the Groucho's waitresses, you wander across the room to where Peter Punchline is chatting to a short, chunky man with a lot of curly dark red hair. The hair is clustered on his scalp, it bursts effusively from his chin in an extravagant beard and peeps provocatively from the open neck of his pink Ralph Lauren tennis shirt.

'Hi,' you say to Punchline. 'I'm Tim Tryer. We met last November when you lectured to my Media Studies group at Redbrick University.'

Punchline, whose chief recollection of the lecture centres around the brunette who tried to sleep her way into television afterwards, can only pretend to recognize you. But don't worry – pretending is enough. And it has the advantage of making the pretender feel at a disadvantage. He introduces you to his companion. 'Tim, this is Nelson Ratings. He used to be my producer at the Beeb, but he's moved to the States as an independent.'

'Absolutely,' concurs Ratings. 'I work out of L.A. most of the time, but I'm pretty much bicoastal.'

At first you think he is referring to his sexual orientation, but it soon becomes clear that Nelson is talking about his professional activities on both the East and West coasts of the USA. Soon the three of you have become engrossed in a conversation on the future of television – a subject upon which your 2.2 in Media Studies gives you every right to pontificate. Amazingly your boyish enthusiasm impresses rather than nauseates Nelson Ratings. Maybe he *is* bicoastal after all.

At any rate, as the party breaks up Punchline suggests you pop into his office at TV Centre later in the week. Then Ratings asks, 'Fancy grabbing a bite to eat somewhere? I have a project I'd like to discuss with you. I could really use a keen young researcher, but I'm flying back tomorrow morning so now's the only time we can talk it over.'

Choices confront you, but your decision depends on your evening so far. If you have already met Lydia Eustace go to 156. If not, try 82.

116

Two weeks later you get a brief note. 'Dear Mr Tryer, Mr Tot has asked me to tell you that he read your letter with interest. However, he feels that it is unduly verbal. This is the age of the image and we at *Barfly, Baffle and Tot* are picture people, not word people. He wishes you the best of luck in another profession and sends his best regards. Yours, Nikki Pout, pp. Tony Tot.'

Tough luck, Tim. But you've still got one more chance. Take your outdated verbals off to *The Cursor*. George Dustjacket can still give you some work at 80.

117

Vanessa Freezeframe turns out to be a brisk career woman in her mid-thirties. She is, she explains, a director of Nothing Special, a satellite TV production company that is looking for new ideas and new faces. Both are in short supply.

As a young author who has clearly got a gift for telly, you could succeed in both categories. And you could make a lot of money doing it.

The thing is, she has to fly off to spend the weekend taking meetings in L.A., but while she's away perhaps you could be thinking about a problem she's got with her latest venture – the search for the ultimate chat-show host. Put your thinking cap on and head off to 164.

118

You spend the night with Camilla, but although you make love to her, frankly it isn't much fun. You're not at your best and she's too far gone. When you part the next morning you swap telephone numbers, but you both know that you are unlikely ever to use them. Until, that is, you turn to 73.

119

You are sent to the Scrubs, where you share a cell designed for two Victorian felons with five other men and a slops bucket. Had you been caught smuggling heroin out of Turkey and incarcerated in the worst that Istanbul had to offer, you could not be forced to endure more primitive conditions. Your fellow-inmates in the cell are a choice collection of perverts, retards and psychopaths. They regard the arrival of an innocent young creature such as yourself as a gift from the gods.

The exact nature of the bestial and degrading acts in which you are forced to participate during your sentence is too repellent to describe here. Simply imagine your worst sexual nightmare. Now double it.

Five years after your fateful evening you are released from jail. You go back home to Drabworthy both mentally and physically starved, barely recognizable as the bright young man who set off to London to make his fortune. Soon after you arrive home – your parents having reluctantly agreed to take you in (you damn near broke your mother's heart, your father informs you) – you begin to suffer night sweats, loss of weight and symptoms of influenza. Terrible rashes and sores break out on your skin.

After so much misfortune you have one, small, piece of luck. Rather than let you linger on for years, the disease is mercifully fast. Your general health has been ruined by jail. You are no match for a determined virus. Six months after returning to Drabworthy . . . you are dead. ☠

120

You wake to find the members of the houseparty bent over you. 'I think he's awake,' says Sophie. 'Good,' says Henry Cornice. 'Now we can kill the bloody rat.' The infuriated Sloanes set to work with a will, kicking, punching, spitting and gouging at your body. Desperately trying to protect your face from the blows raining down upon it, you struggle to your feet and run off to your room. You pack up all your gear and head for the exit. At the foot of the stairs a lynch-mob awaits. Sophie has by now collapsed in tears.

'Look what you've done, you bastard,' snarls Cornice. 'You've killed a harmless old dog. You've wrecked the Lymeswolds' garden, and you've made poor Sophie cry. You're not welcome here. And we don't want to find you at Sophie's house when we get back to town. Why don't you go back to the grotty little town you came from. Crawl back under your stone, you proley shit.'

I think you can take it that you've blown it. You are blackballed from young London society. Word of your atrocities spreads to the point where no one wants to have you in their home. You spend a few weeks in a humble bedsit struggling to make ends meet, but the power of the social Mafia is overwhelming. All the more so when Johnny Standfirst tips off the tabloids to 'TIM TRYER ATE MY LABBY.'

There is no future for you in London. There isn't much future anywhere. Go back to Drabworthy. And don't come back. ☠

121

Lydia smiles as you walk over to her and gestures that she'll meet you outside. You've been waiting on the pavement for five minutes, wondering whether she's about to stand you up, when she appears beside you, pecks your cheek and takes your arm. 'I'm so sorry,' she says. 'I didn't want anyone to see us leave together. The place was crawling with gossip columnists.'

You dine together in a tiny Chinese restaurant in Soho. You are the only Westerners there, but the manager beams and shows you to Lydia's regular corner table. You hardly notice what you eat – all your concentration is focused on Lydia and hers on you. There is an electric current flowing between you. Your heart is pounding, you can scarcely breathe for the passion building up between you.

That first night, spent in a frenzy of sexual ecstasy in the bedroom, in the bath, on the drawing-room rug of Lydia's Islington flat, sets a pattern for the next six months. Your vague attempts to get a job occupy a tiny part of your time, but it is Lydia who obsesses you. You have never known love like this. Your world revolves around her. Eventually she has to leave the country for three weeks' filming in Italy. Before you can join her there you receive a card. She has met, fallen in love with and married a cameraman. She thanks you for the past few months. She'll never forget you. She wants to be friends. Sophie Godyah-Raleigh finds your body the next morning. You have washed down all Sonya's sleeping pills with a bottle of Jamie's whisky. A letter to Lydia is found beside you, but since nobody knows her address in Italy it is thrown away. After the coroner has delivered a verdict of suicide, your parents come to take your body back to Drabworthy. You never have the chance to read the headline that brings your fifteen minutes of fame. 'TV GIRL'S TOY BOY IN PILL DEATH LOVE-PACT,' it reads.

122

You can hardly control yourself as you wait to hear how the programme went down with the public. Go to 180.

123

You refuse the job at the BBC because it seems too early for you to get stuck in a bureaucracy. When you're young and talented you can step in at the top simply because you don't know the 'right' way to go about getting there. Plodding on a hierarchical ladder doesn't seem your style.

George Dustjacket, literary editor of *The Cursor*, who lives in the basement at Barchester Gardens, agrees. He thinks you should move around and try various things. He suggests you pay the bills in the meantime by sub-editing: if you can concentrate, recognize a sentence and use a telephone and dictionary you can be a sub, says George. He arranges some casual shifts on the arts pages of *The Cursor* for you. Go to 80.

124

You throw your toothbrush and a spare pair of socks into a Sainsbury's plastic bag and pile into Sophie's Golf GTi. Sophie provides heart-stopping driving over to Stoke Newington where you pick up Sonya and two others: VICTORIA MELVILLE-LENNOX-BARCLAY-STEWART, a colleague of Sophie's from the gallery Wildebeest De Trop, where she has a decorative function usually performed by a rubber plant in less sophisticated businesses, and the HON. HENRY CORNICE, house painter and the despair of his parents who feel that thirty-two is rather old to be still living at home.

On the journey down to Cambridgeshire, Henry offers you a Red Stripe Crucial Brew from his crate of cans on the back window – he finds drinking much easier than conversation. You find drinking much easier than sobriety when Sophie is driving, and conversation is impossible anyway as the volume of The Proclaimers on the cassette player dislodges the catarrh in your sinuses. In the crush of the back seat, however, body-language speaks cosily through extensive leg-contact with the attractive Victoria.

Arriving temporarily deafened at Slythemere at 9.00 p.m, you find the lights already shining through the mullioned windows of the Lymeswolds' early-19th century pile. Sophie informs you that her step-brother OLIVER LYMESWOLD, has been down here for some weeks, recuperating after his much-publicized three month prison sentence for trying to smuggle his pet sloth Cecil into Britain.

You make his acquaintance over huge quantities of spag bol in the kitchen. He relates his experiences in the Amazon and Strangeways in between large amounts of excellent Burgundy, courtesy of Sir Nicholas Lymeswold, the lock of whose cellars Oliver finally picked this afternoon. Sophie lavishes kisses and hugs on her ancient incontinent half-blind labrador, wittily known as 'Labby', who sniffs everyone's crotch and whines for pickings from the table. Sophie is shocked when you suggest putting her out of the kitchen. By 11.00 p.m. everyone round the table is completely plastered: Henry is swapping maudlin memories of prep school with Oliver, Sonya tearfully explains the current setback in her love-life to a near catatonic Sophie, and Victoria giggles seductively at your collection of knock-knock jokes. Go to 75.

125

Your time spent with The Idle Rich enables you to do a brilliant article on them, spiced with the sort of inside gossip that no journalist would ever normally be able to unearth. Charlotte Van Dryver is delighted. She wants to give you a new commission as soon as possible. It seems that she hasn't been able to find anyone else either good enough or cheap enough to write the left-handers piece. You've turned it down once, but after Charlotte has offered you an extra couple of hundred quid it seems like a better idea than you originally thought. Go to 177 and get reporting.

126

As you scan the room you spot a face that you really do know. It belongs to PETER PUNCHLINE, a top TV sitcom writer whom you met when he came to lecture to your university Media Studies group on writing for television. Just when you are about to go over to where he is chatting to another middle-aged man, you spot Lydia. She has swapped the crinolines and petticoats of Victorian England for a look that is startlingly up to date. Her slender, honey-tanned physique has been poured into a clinging jersey dress by Azzedine Alaia that is cut and stitched to show her every curve to best advantage. Her tawny hair tumbles about her shoulders. Her long legs are almost entirely uncovered by her hip-high skirt. Yes, she's *that* fabulous.

Your head says you haven't a chance with Lydia. Go to 115

and see if you can start a professionally advantageous conversation with Mr Punchline and his chum.

Your groin says that Lydia Eustace is the most gorgeous girl you have ever seen. Throw yourself at her mercy at 6.

Brains or balls? The choice is yours.

127

That last drink you downed may well have been a tactical error. As you stagger off home you gradually become aware that both your mind and body have come under severe alcoholic assault. Amidst the general sense of discomfort you can distinguish two principal problems. These are (a) that the pavement on which you are walking has acquired all the stability of the bridge of the Herald of Free Enterprise and (b) that you desperately need to take a leak.

There's no way that you can last out till you get home, particularly since there's no sign of a taxi or night bus anywhere. But on your right you can dimly make out a dark and apparently deserted alley. If you just sneak in there and relieve yourself against the wall you'll soon feel a lot better.

Cheered by the thought that the pain of self-control will soon give way to the ecstasy of release, you meander gently into the alley. The fate that awaits you there will be revealed at 52.

128

After ten minutes you begin to come round to the immediate implications of your act. You rapidly decide that you cannot leave things as they are and just explain to Sophie what has happened. Weakened by alcohol and remorse, you don't feel mentally strong enough to face her without a complete personality breakdown. If you decide to flee back to London, go to 749. If you would rather hide the evidence of your deed and brazen it out, go to 9.

129

Chastened by your experience of close contact with women beyond your station (you can just imagine your Mum back in Drabworthy warning you about fast society girls) you retreat to Barchester Gardens to plan your next move. Over the next few weeks you strike up a friendship with George Dustjacket, the Literary Editor who lives in the basement. Dustjacket is books supremo at *The Cursor*, the brand-new, Brixton-based, computer-operated quality newspaper whose accuracy, impartiality and highfalutin' tedium are generally reckoned to have restored cherished traditional values to Britain's corrupted journalism. Taking pity on your poverty and unemployment, he makes a couple of suggestions to you. Would you like to do a few shifts on the Arts pages of *The Cursor*? Or perhaps, he suggests, you're not really cut out for such a worthy, but low-key job. A chap like you, with his eye on the main chance, might be better suited to another business – how about advertising? Dustjacket is still on excellent terms with his ex-brother-in-law TONY TOT, who is not only the father of the outspoken fourteen-year-old style columnist TERRY TOT, but also the MD of *Barfly, Baffle and Tot*, currently London's most go-go agency following their outstanding work for the Monster Raving Loony Party.

If you'd rather die than go and prostitute your soul in advertising, *The Cursor* is at 80. But if you think you'd look rather good in red-framed glasses, check out Tony Tot at 159.

130

Oh no, this is too bad. You're so close to the end you can practically taste all the wonderful things that are waiting for you there. And then this had to happen. What can we say? We're distraught. It's just terrible to have to say this, but – hell, you know how it is – *que sera sera*.

The truth is, you were coming back to London from the country. You had that great idea for the TV show you were going to do with Vanessa Freezeframe. If you'd played your cards right it could have been the single most popular TV show in the world.

So it's terribly, terribly sad to have to say that your car hit some black ice on the motorway. You were doing 120 m.p.h. You didn't stand a chance. But wow, the wake they had for you at The Nightclub was really something else. Everyone was there. In fact, that's where Vanessa decided to get Terry Tot to do the show instead. That's showbiz, eh, Tim old sport? ☠

131

You crawler. Your piece is well written, but soft. Charlotte Van Dryver publishes it, but lets you know that *Malice* would rather run pieces with a lot more bite in them. It's clear that your chances of getting many more commissions in the near future are somewhat limited.

But there is some good news. At least two of your subjects are the kinds of people who deal in rose-tinted, sycophantic and quite possibly misleading prose. They are, of course, Des Res, the property developer and Tony Tot, the advertising executive. Both find that all their friends ring up and congratulate them, they are treated with new respect at their golf clubs and their wives bring back glowing reports from their hairdressers. If your prose can have this effect on their private lives, they calculate, perhaps it could be good for their business too. So within ten days of the article's publication both have rung you up inviting you to come and see them to discuss an exciting professional proposition.

Which career seems the more promising? If you feel that you are at heart an adman, Tony Tot is waiting in his office at 60. But if you are titillated by the vast profits to be had from speculating on the property market — profits that may, who knows, enable you to rival Jamie Pole-Position's prodigious earning power — then Des is your man at 24.

132

Only over your fourth armagnac does Isobel Baskerville finally come clean. Apparently Kunstwerk was impressed by your sarcastic style in *Malice* despite being the one of the objects, and would like to co-write a book with you to be published by Hale & Hearty. His opinions, your writing. Kunstwerk and Baskerville warm to their theme. The working title is *Blowing Up Britain* and it will suggest the 100 buildings we could most do without. The beginning of Kunstwerk's list is uncontroversial: the West London Air Terminal, the Hilton Hotel . . . but rises to a crescendo of condemnation, ending with Anne Hathaway's Cottage, St Paul's Cathedral, Castle Howard and Chequers. Each will be critically demolished, and then suggestions given on how this could be practically achieved – where to plant explosives, weak points, load-bearing walls, inflammable materials . . .

Baskerville waxes rapturously on the commercial potential of the book: she explains that architecture has become the artform for the Eighties, just as film was for the Seventies. Both have good mixes of democratic and elitist tendencies, impressive sounding technical terms and critical jargon. So mix architecture with the Eighties penchant for violence *et voilà* . . . aesthetic terrorism! Baskerville sees US editions, French editions, Japanese, Bulgarian . . . not to mention film rights, TV rights, T-shirt rights, merchandising . . . she is just describing the computer game based on the book when you ask how much Hale & Hearty will pay. She stops short. 'You've got to see it in the long term, Tim . . .' You ask again. She says £6,000.

Between the two of you. Two-thirds going to Kunstwerk. Final payment on publication. You finally work out that in return for writing most of 80,000 words – at least three months' work – you will make £2,000 over eighteen months.

If this grabs you, go to 63. If you think journalism is a better route to money and success, go to 27.

133

You've finished the manuscript at last! And on time! You've just written the final sentence on the concluding description of how three well-placed bombs could bring down Blackpool Tower. The computer printer chugs away and the final pages are placed with the large pile. Then fear overcomes you: the strange occurrences of the last few weeks have left you rather paranoid. It is possible that someone is keen on your book not reaching the British Public – possibly the British Government. You have the only manuscript in your hands now. It suddenly becomes imperative that you have several copies.

You leave Barchester Gardens intending to go to the Instant Print shop at South Kensington tube. You lock the door and turn to see across the road the now familiar figure who always seems to be loitering around your house. This time instead of avoiding your eye he looks straight at you and waves, indicating you should cross over to him.

What do you do? If you want ignore him and carry on and photocopy your precious manuscript, go to 31.

If you want to cross the road to meet the mysterious stranger, go to 162.

134

You arrange to see Naomi the next day at the Southwark offices of Brute Features, the independent company which is making *A Kick Up The Arts* for Channel 4. You meet the commissioning editors and make a good impression on them. This may lead to big things.

In the meantime they would like you to prepare an eight-minute film report on travel writing. The hook for this is that three leading travel writers are producing new works in the next couple of months. Interviews with F. T. COMMENT, STANISLAUS NURISTAN and INGRID REFERENCE have been arranged.

Grab a film crew and an expenses sheet and go to 17.

135

The one person who has stood by you through all this is Johnny Standfirst. As Sophie Godyah-Raleigh once suggested, he has essentially liberal principles. He doesn't care whether you did what you were accused of or not, he just sees you as a victim of repression. He says that he knows one person who might be able to help you. She's called VANESSA FREEZEFRAME and she runs a TV production company called Obscure Opinions that makes a leftish current affairs programme on Channel 4.

You are introduced to Vanessa over dinner at a vegetarian restaurant and are delighted to find that here is someone to whom your recent experiences count as a distinct professional advantage. Her only complaint is that you aren't actually gay, in which case you could be seen as part of a victimized minority instead of just plain victimized. But even so, she feels strongly enough about your case to want to do something about it.

As she sees it, she has two options she can offer you. She could make a film about your case, which would make a strong lead item for an edition of the Obscure Opinions' programme and might very well mobilize public opinion in your favour. She's certain that she could get several Opposition MPs to take her findings to the Home Secretary. The story of how an innocent young man's life was ruined – it would be great television and have wonderful follow-up potential. But if you feel that you've had enough unpleasant publicity already she can, she thinks, find you a job as a researcher on the show. You have a media studies degree and some experience – that should be enough. The pay's not brilliant, but it's a start.

Which do you think sounds like the better idea? If you see yourself as a potential *cause celebre*, Vanessa will start filming at 83. If you want a job, it's at 72.

136

You can't take Kelly-Marie with you to the Seychelles, but that's no problem because you've been two-timing her in any case, so you've got a travelling reserve. She's NIKKI POUT, who happens to be Tony Tot's secretary. You met when you were doing the left-handers piece for *Malice* and you've been running a pretty successful campaign with her ever since. Nikki hasn't got a brain in her body and she's the kind of girl who goes off for a weekend in the country with four pairs of stilettos and no boots, but as far as you're concerned that's her charm. You long ago abandoned the notions about women that you had when you came down from Redbrick – that they were equal partners in an intelligent, caring relationship. That kind of wishy-washy liberal stuff hardly fits with the lifestyle that you enjoy – and boy, do you enjoy it – now. Sod the credibility, you're thinking, give me more ecstasy.

Sure, have as much as you want. It won't do you any good. On your third day by the sea, alarmed by the lustful looks that the other guys on the beach are casting at Nikki, who responds with a series of increasingly diminutive monokinis, you decide to prove your machismo to her.

You grab a windsurfer and ignore the warnings of the lifeguard as you speed out towards the reefs. You're planning a series of outrageous stunts – flips and somersaults with an astounding degree of difficulty, executed with maximum artistic interpretation. You're wasting your time. Nikki isn't paying the slightest bit of attention. She's mesmerizing the beach with her own routine. Ten minutes on her front, her sandy, perfectly rounded bum twitching provocatively as her bee-stung lips wrap themselves around the words of the Jackie Collins blockbuster she's pretending to read. Then a flip of her own – onto her back, so the world can see her coffee-tanned breasts standing to attention beneath the tropical sun.

No one's watching, not even the lifeguard, when the wind and the currents combine to sweep you helplessly out beyond the reefs and into the Indian Ocean. It's an hour or more before Nikki even notices you're gone and by then it's far too late. In a desperate attempt to get back to shore you dive off the windsurfer and try to swim the half mile or so back to the beach. Softened by a regular diet of expense-account lunches you would be hard-pressed to swim half a mile in a swimming pool. In an ocean, battling against waves and tides, you have no chance at all. Death by drowning is not a pleasant way to go. But you would happily exchange it for your actual fate, which becomes all-too inevitable when you spot the grey-black triangles circling you in the water.

Although your windsurfer is later recovered by some fisherman your death goes unreported. Well, no one wants to disturb the tourists. Nikki is upset at first, but then – brave girl – she decides to go out and enjoy herself. She's sure, she tells the boys, you would have wanted it that way. ☠

137

You make it back to London by lunchtime, half expecting to be arrested as you arrive at Barchester Gardens. A strategy for dealing with the consequences forms in your mind, but in the meantime you need something to occupy you. Johnny Standfirst's offer for the clashing demos still stands and you decide to take him up. Go to 172.

You arrive at Hamish Urquhart's dinner well after nine o'clock. Your mother would be appalled by such tardiness – in Drabworthy they would have finished the Black Forest gateau and be well into the After Eights by now. But things don't work quite like that in Sloane Rangerland. Since most of the men work in the City and stay at their desks at least until seven o'clock, it's gone half-eight by the time they're ready to think about a spot of dinner. Hamish isn't cooking, of course. He's had a couple of Carolines he knows who run a catering service called Super Suppers bring round their standard dealers' dinner; cold cucumber soup, Beef Wellington with new potatoes and *mange tout*, and chocolate mousse to finish.

The food is, naturally, secondary to the drink at these occasions. In fact, you begin to wonder whether you aren't involved in an upper-class party game. Its rules are: everyone has to bring a bottle of wine, drink that and then down anything the host has provided. The last guest standing wins. In the event of a tie the winner is the contestant who can still remember his own name.

Having thought of this little quip you are keen to try it out on one of the girls on either side of you. To your left is a good-looking blonde with a reckless aristocratic manner and a face you recognize from Dempster and the society pages of the glossy magazines. She's introduced to you by Sophie as 'Killer' but it doesn't take you long to work out that this is the HON. CAMILLA SOMETHING, daughter of LORD WHATNOT, the prominent Catholic peer and owner of Whatnot Hall, a Palladian jewel set in 5,000 acres of rolling Oxfordshire countryside and hung with a priceless collection of Constables, Rembrandts and Vermeers.

To your right is a thin, intense girl in her late twenties with a tight, narrow mouth and a severe crop of dark mouse hair. She is wearing a black suit with a short, tight skirt that suggests efficiency, rather than sexuality. She introduces herself as CHARLOTTE VAN DRYVER, but you miss her job description in the general blare of conversation. You think she said something about a magazine. At a guess you might reckon she was the editor's secretary. She has that slightly officious air about her.

So who will better appreciate your wit? Turn to Camilla Something at 36. Or try it on with Charlotte Van Dryver at 94.

139

You wait anxiously to hear what your colleagues feel about your choice. Go to 142.

140

A very sensible choice. Your flat is expensive, but it is in an excellent area and is a sound conversion. You gain social credibility because your friends can easily get to you for dinner, or drop in after a Saturday morning exploring the market on the Portobello Road. Your frequent appearances at 192 – that's a restaurant, not the number of a section of this book – mark you out as a discerning diner. Best of all is the steady appreciation that sends the value of your flat rising towards the £120,000 mark. You can now devote your full attention to you work in the safe knowledge that, should you ever be short of a bob or two, you can sell your home and raise a helluva lot of money.

So get back to your career. Proceed to 110 immediately.

141

The waste of time and effort in this aborted book project appals you, but you plunge back into work determined to make up for lost time. At Barchester Gardens you spend more time drinking whisky in the evenings with basement occupant George Dustjacket, Literary Editor of *The Cursor*. Knowing that you are looking for money and seeking new challenges, he offers you some shifts on his pages – a bit boring, but possibly a way into the newspaper business. Go to 80.

142

In fact it doesn't make any difference which selection of celebrities you choose. These are easily the least important items in *Idol Chatter*. What do guests matter? They're just camera fodder. What does matter is the image you present to the world: your clothes, your hair, your accent.

Which of the following do you choose:

Paul Smith suit, severely razored flat-top, Sarf Lunnon accent (*scuola di* Robert Elms, 163).

Katherine Hamnett suit, dyed blond hair, David Hockney hornrims, Yorkshire accent, 154.

Scott Crolla suit, severe skinhead, Gorbals accent, 122.

143

It's five minutes before your one o'clock lunch date with Charlotte Van Dryver. Her assistant called yesterday to tell you a table was booked at the killingly fashionable Soho restaurant, Au Dessus De Sa Gare, and now you're sitting there in the corner of the first floor dining-room.

Opposite, you notice the predatory Antipodean TV arts presenter SYDNEY DARWIN ('the lizard of Oz') with one of his natural prey, publishing PR BELINDA PROMO. In the far corner, literary agent Piers Halfcut is lunching his third-best client, schlock romance writer BRONWEN HEILBRON, author of *How Green Was My Judgement*. At the large central table are four members of 'the glossy posse' of fashion pundits and stylists. This elegant coven, tightly and expensively tailored in black, are engaged in their favourite pastime of flaying a reputation alive – this time FELIX DE CATTE, New York editor of *Croque Monsieur*. They fall silent as the editor of *Malice* sweeps in, greets them briefly, greets you, sits down, scans the menu rapidly and asks you if you're ready to order.

After the earlier establishment of your hip credentials with the details of Zagreb nightlife, you have to keep up the cool credibility with your choice of courses.

If you want *Prawn Cocktail*, *Steak* and *Pommes Frites* and House Claret, go to 30.

If *Gravad Lax, Brochette de Lotte* and Californian Chardonnay, go to 89.

If *Sorrel Soup, Salade Tiede*, and *Badoit* mineral water, go to 65.

144

Sophie is not overwhelmed to hear from you again – you were *saaach* a drag when you were ill. But she perks up considerably when you say you want to take her out to celebrate your recent financial success. After an evening of considerable wallet abuse, one dinner at Chez Guevara, two magnums of Dom Perignon, three night clubs and four lines of cocaine, a highly-animated Sophie throws her arms around you in the back of a cab and says of course you must come back and live in her house.

Next day you wake at lunch and lightly bandage your hangover with a handful of painkillers. You spend all afternoon recuperating. At 7.00 you arrive at Barchester Gardens with a bunch of roses, another magnum for Sophie – and your luggage.

Go to 103.

145

A slight hush falls on the people around you. You, a total stranger, have just propositioned one of Britain's most brilliant and beautiful young actresses. Sonya, who heard what you said, rushes up to her friend in embarrassment. 'Oh God, Lydia darling, I'm *so* sorry. I'm afraid Tim's new to town, he doesn't really know what he's saying.' Then she flashes you a killing look – you have clearly let her down in front of people she needs to impress.

You wish the ground would swallow you up. Lydia looks at you, her blue eyes cool and clear. She hesitates a fraction, then a tiny smile appears at the corner of her full, inviting mouth. 'Oh, I don't know, Sonya. I think he's rather sweet.'

The tension that had been created in the room dissolves into a happy hubbub of conversation. Nobody notices as Lydia leans forward and whispers in your ear, 'Don't leave without me.'

Congratulations, Tim, that was a stroke of pure genius. Now see if you can advance your professional career as well by talking to Peter Punchline at 115.

146

For a second the policeman's attention is on his radio and not on you. So you burst up off the ground and run for your life down the alley. But dissipation has taken its toll and you're no match for a sober cop. Before you can get twenty yards he has caught up with you and sent you crashing with a rugby tackle.

He pulls you roughly to your feet. Then he snarls at you, 'You cheeky little bastard. I'm going to have to teach you to be still, like a good little boy.' And he knees you, hard, in the groin.

'Have you learned your lesson?' he asks, kicking your legs from under you. As you land in a heap on the pavement you cry out that, yes, you have. But by now physical torture has given way to mental. Your mind is bursting with fear, panic and indignation. 'You can't do this to me,' you plead. 'I haven't done anything wrong.'

'Oh yes you have,' he replies. 'Try gross indecency and assaulting a police officer for starters. And there'll be a lot more by the time we're finished.'

Before your conversation – if it can be called that – can go any further, the night is split by the sound of a wailing police siren. A few seconds later the alley is filled with a whirling blue light as a van pulls up at its junction with the street. Four more policemen charge from it, pick you up and fling you in the back. The rear doors close and the van is off again, taking you to your destination at 68.

147

Over the course of the late afternoon and evening, Sonya and Johnny return from their weekend expeditions. Jamie has Concorded off to New York to check out a nightclub a friend recommended and will be going straight into his office from the airport on Monday morning.

Sonya has been staying with friends in Wiltshire and spent the morning walking around the stones at Avebury circle. She is impressed by your knowledge of Neolithic Britain, largely formed from vague memories of BBC2 *Chronicle* programmes and hippy-ish paperbacks, but presented in your confident, plausible manner. The Brownie points you gain with Sonya stand you in good stead when, half-an-hour later, you confess your undying lust for the actress playing Nancy in the latest BBC adaptation of *Oliver Twist*. It happens to be on the TV that is sitting – on, but unwatched – in the corner of the drawing-room.

Underwhelmed as Sonya is by your feelings for another actress, particularly one of her own generation who is more successful than herself, she is decent enough to say that the actress – LYDIA EUSTACE – is a close friend of hers. In fact, she'll probably be seeing her at a party on Tuesday. Would you like to come along?

Sure, you say, if some work doesn't turn up I'd love to.

Later the same evening Johnny, who has learned of your ambitions in journalism, mentions that he thinks the Diary column of the national paper for which he works occasionally is looking for an editorial assistant. It might be a good job with which to start. Why don't you meet him on Tuesday for a drink after his reporting shift finishes and talk it all over with someone from the Diary. You say you'll do your best.

On Monday morning Sophie, who spent Sunday evening in a marathon hair-wash, pedicure and face-mask session – thereby missing your conversations with Sonya and Johnny – mentions that she's going to a dinner-party on Tuesday night. The host is HAMISH URQUHART. 'You'd *really* like him,' Sophie says.

'*He's so* nice and he's *incredibly* clever. I'll call him. I'm sure he won't mind if you come too.'

What Sophie means by 'incredibly clever' is that Hamish got a Third in Land Economy at a Cambridge College where intelligence counted for less than connections. Or perhaps she's referring to the considerable skill he displayed picking winners at Newmarket, which was where he spent most of his undergraduate time. Her real purpose in taking you is to use you as a smokescreen behind which she can pursue her ambition of getting Hamish (a) into bed and (b) into church. Even so, the dinner could be fun.

So make your choice. If you fancy the chance of meeting Lydia Eustace, turn to 29.

If you'd rather have a drink with Johnny and his newspaper contact, wet your whistle at 79.

Alternatively, go to dinner with Sophie at 138.

148

You wash your hair, shave four times, put on your best suit and make sure that you get to the studio with an hour to spare. Rose gives you an idea of the questions that you will be asked and even rehearses a few amusing replies.

So when it is time for you to go on-stage and face Terry Wogan, you are as relaxed as a young man making his television debut live before several million people could ever be expected to be.

Both Wogan and the audience are charmed by your wit, your articulacy, your modest self-deprecation at any mention of the quality of your book. After the show the producer makes a special point of congratulating you and asking you to come back again in a few months' time. Rose, too, is delighted. Your success has made her look good for suggesting you. The two of you go to dinner feeling on top of the world.

You wake up the next morning, give Rose a fond kiss, nuzzle around her ear and down the back of her neck, and go out to fetch coffee and the papers. Both your book and your appearance on Wogan get mentions and reviews – all glowing. The only bad news all morning is Rose's confession that she is actually engaged to a fantastically wealthy Venezuelan banker who flies in from Caracas that afternoon. But no sooner has this disappointment registered than the phone rings.

It's a woman's voice on the line. 'Hullo, Tim Tryer? You don't know me, but my name is VANESSA FREEZEFRAME. I work for a satellite television company and I saw you on *Wogan* last night. I'd very much like to meet you. I think it might be very good for both of us. My office is just off Oxford Street. Do you think you could make it by, say, ten-thirty?'

Good Lord, she must be serious, it's already half-nine now. If you want to meet Ms Freezeframe, go to her office at 117. But if you'd rather spend your morning trying to persuade the beautiful Rose to stay with you, pour out your heart to her at 71.

149

Your parents are appalled when you show them around your new home. It's small, dark, clearly suffering from several exciting forms of rot, some of them previously unknown to science, and it is in a very, very rough area indeed.

The house needs a lot of work (it was somewhat cheaper than either the wardrobe in Knightsbridge or the flat in Notting Hill because of its unconverted condition). But, as the agent pointed out, this only means that you can bring your own stamp to the conversion and make it so very much more individually *yours*.

Within a week someone has left their stamp on your car and made the radio-cassette very much more theirs than it was before. The insurance covers the broken window and scratched paintwork, but you have to pay for the new Blaupunkt, and the one after that.

When the builders come round to give their estimates they look around, rub their chins, scratch their heads, exhale despondently a couple of times and then quote figures that blow your mind. 'You'll be completely fixed up for, what, twelve grand?' the agent had ventured. Well, not one of the estimates is under £18K, and that's without the cost of the kitchen and bathroom fittings.

Finally you narrow the choice of contractors down to two. One of them, Mounting and Joist Ltd, are a highly respected firm who handle building work all over the South-East. But they're expensive, £24,500, and they won't be free for a month. On the other hand, Mr O'Mallet from down the road, with his three boys Mel, Del and Tel, reckons he can save five grand on that, easy. And he can start tomorrow.

Which do you choose? The respectable builders are at 37. The Irish are having a drink at 158.

150

You prudish, double-standard holder, you! You've had no previous qualms about clodhoppingly propositioning young women.

Vanessa Freezeframe takes your refusal with good grace. 'Another time, perhaps.'

On your bike later that afternoon, your attention is distracted at Piccadilly Circus by an attractive and (you think) familiar face, the actress Lydia Eustace. You make another circuit in order to see her more closely but inadvertently get in the path of a frustrated Geordie lorry driver who took the wrong turn crossing the Thames and has been averaging 1½ mph for the past two hours. He accelerates to change lanes and you find yourself crushed between the truck and a Mr Softee ice-cream van.

Your demise merits four lines on page two of the *Evening Standard* the next day – but only the first edition. Your mention is squeezed out on the Midday Prices by an Associated Press report on the world's largest aubergine, just grown in Azerbeijan. ☠

151

At Hale & Hearty's offices the following morning you discover a worried group: Lazlo Kunstwerk, your co-writer; Isobel Baskerville, your editor; and two men introduced to you as Miles Binding, the chairman of the publishers, and Toby Brief, their solicitor. The reason for this meeting is revealed to you. *Blowing Up Britain* has found itself the object of considerable disapproval by HMG. An exchange of letters with the Attorney General has led to a final warning that if publication goes ahead publishers, printers, distributors and particularly the authors will be liable for prosecution for, among other charges, incitement to terrorism, incitement to cause damage to property, conspiracy to cause damage, conspiracy to commit arson, etc.

Toby Brief explains that if the case comes to court and you are convicted you could be banged up for a stretch of time more easily expressed in scientific notation (1.749×10^3).

Brief is counselling caution, but Miles Binding seems more gung-ho than not (as befits a man responsible for Hale & Harty's success of the previous season – an illustrated pop-up book of Peter Wright's *Spycatcher*). Lazlo and Isobel seem to be looking to you for a lead.

It is explained that it really now comes down to you and Lazlo: do you want to risk lifelong prison food and gang rape for £6,000? If you do, go to 2.

If you would rather drop it, take the money offered by Miles Binding and return to your journalistic career, go to 141.

152

You are living from a suitcase and pursued by journalists. After a few weeks your health breaks down. Melancholia strikes you as well as physical weakness. You try to go home to rest but your parents (*Daily Mail* readers) have disowned you as a revolting degenerate. In despair in an Ealing bedsit you swallow a bottle of aspirins and wash them down with a bottle of The Glenlivet (you always lived big). However, a writ-server from Ingrid Reference, who took great exception to your views on her travel writing, has tracked you down to Ealing and arrives in time to call an ambulance. He tucks the writ into your trouser pocket as they take you off to pump your stomach.

You leave hospital still ill and depressed, but the press has lost its interest in you and at least you're not a wanderer any more. The Social Services department has found you a hard-to-let council flat in a tower block in the depths of the East End, Barrow Marshes E18. Go to 109.

153

Unfortunately the dollar goes to $1.65 and you find yourself with £12,500 worth of useless contracts. You blew it. Depression sets in again and bad health recurs. You fall further and further into the underclass in Reginald Maudling House. You are electrocuted one evening as, soggy with British sherry, you kick in the TV after an advertisement for unit trusts appeared. As a legal requirement the ad stated, 'REMEMBER INVESTMENTS CAN GO DOWN AS WELL AS UP.' ☠

154

The Yorkshire voice, the dyed hair, the Hockney style, it's all just a little . . . *camp*. One of the crueller reviewers says you come across like Larry Grayson's niece. After three episodes, each of which shows a significant decline in ratings, you are dropped. Agents and producers hardly fall over themselves in their attempts to get you on to other programmes and you are consigned to that special limbo reserved for failed chat-show hosts.

Hard luck, Tim, so near and yet so far. It's funny, isn't it, how some people just don't seem to have what it takes? ☠

155

You get to New York on a super-cheap bucket shop flight for which you have to provide your own food, in-flight entertainment and seat cushions. It lands at an airport in the wilds of New Jersey. So you take a bus into Manhattan and then have to make your way to your friend's apartment. You've only got ten dollars and the clothes you stand up in. No way can you afford a cab. Better go to 50 and take the subway.

156

Nelson Ratings' invitation has put you in a bit of a spot. The chance of a job with an international TV company is a dream come true. On the other hand, Lydia is looking at you from the far side of the room. It is clear that she is about to leave and that she wants you to come with her. The chance of a night with Lydia Eustace is a wet dream come true.

Nelson is eating at 69. Lydia's moving on to 121.

Your club, christened simply 'Nightclub', is a fantastic success. Every night you stand by the door for a while just for the pleasure of watching the smartest people in town beg and bribe the doormen in the hope of being granted the chance to spend £25 on the entrance fee. One night you turn away David Bowie, the Duchess of York, Madonna and Sean Penn – all before midnight.

From your point of view things couldn't be better. Whenever a journalist or TV crew want a comment on the club – roughly every seventeen minutes – you are on hand to give one. You soon become the best-known nightclub impresario in London, much to the fury of all the others, who are rapidly losing their custom.

The power that you wield as the arbiter of social failure or

triumph at Nightclub's door makes you fabulously attractive to women. *Malice* profile you over several pages, with photographs by Snowdon. 'By the way,' says Lord S. after the session, 'my children asked me to ask you; do you think you could get them tickets for Nightclub tonight?' You're feeling generous – yeah, sure, David and Sarah can come along anytime. Why not?

One of your most regular punters is VANESSA FREEZE-FRAME, a television producer who runs an independent company – Nothing Special – who are heavily involved in global satellite TV. You can use her. She likes to be able to get in the club and impress her contacts. You both find each other attractive enough to be seen with. Naturall you start an affair, although (what with your respective positions) you agree not to do anything untill the medical tests are done. In the meantime, you know Vanessa is looking for the ultimate in chat-shows, – surely among all the stylish people who come to the Nightclub you could find the ultimate chat-show host. Put your thinking cap on and go to [164].

158

O'Mallet and the boys turn up three weeks late, having had a little spot of bother on a job – well, more of a favour for a friend, really – they were doing down Chorley way. They smash down a couple of walls, disconnect all the drains, leave the guttering in heaps outside the front door and then disappear for two weeks. You can't ever seem to get through to them on the telephone. You can't flush the loo or empty a bath, and every time it rains the water pours down the walls of the house and streams in through the holes that were supposed to be fixed by now.

When work actually starts in earnest your life establishes a regular routine of misery. Every morning at eight Mel, Del and Tel arrive, drink a lot of your coffee and settle down to do *The Sun* crossword. They are still straining over this challenging intellectual exercise when you leave the house for work at nine. Indeed, there's little to suggest that they ever manage to get through an entire puzzle, or do anything else at all except drink even more coffees and three pints each at lunch, because when you come back in the evening the place looks exactly the same as it did before, except that it might be even more chaotic. Then O'Mallet calls to say there's been some sort of problem. He's going to need an RSJ, a new damp course, a complete set of floor joists, new doors, tiles, plaster, bricks and so forth. Could you leave some cash for him in the morning?

My God, is it going to go on like this forever? Find out at 114.

159

Dustjacket puts in a good word for you with Tot, who suggests over the phone that you put something down on paper. 'Tell me about yourself,' he says. 'Give me the psychographics. I want your dreams, your hopes, your aspirations. Are you a *Barfly, Baffle and Tot* kind of guy. Believe me, Tim, I want to know.'

You sit down and write the finest 2,000 words you have ever penned. Everything is in there – the whole hejira from Drabworthy to Barchester Gardens and beyond. Maybe you shouldn't send it to Tot. Maybe you should submit it for publication instead.

Just as you are about to post this tome another thought strikes you: what if he doesn't like it? A busy man like Tot might not have the time to wade through a ten-page job application. You try another tack. You go to a photo booth and take a moody black-and-white shot of yourself. This you take to a processing lab and have blown up to the size of a newspaper page. Then, in Letraset, you add the words, 'Timothy Tryer. Timothy Writer. Timothy Lover. Timothy Achiever.' At the bottom is your phone number.

It looks vain, pretentious and meaningless. But it's short. So which application do you send? If you'd go with the letter, try 116. If the poster's more your style, pin it up on 60.

160

You wait anxiously to hear what your colleagues feel about your choice. Go to 142.

161

Did you cheat? Have you noticed? You see, no matter what your opening line to Lydia you end up in exactly the same place. Here. The reason is simple. Pick-up lines are to a greater or lesser degree immaterial. The chances are that Lydia, like almost any other woman at this or any other party, has made up her mind about you before you've even opened your mouth. If she's picked up good vibes, if she thinks you look good, and if her subconscious is hit by the correct pheromones it doesn't matter what you say. If it's good she'll be impressed. If it's crass she'll be amused. She'll probably tease you about it in bed one day. But if the signals are wrong . . . buddy, you could be Shakespeare – it wouldn't do you any good.

So what does Lydia think. Toss a coin. If you get heads, go to 40. If you get tails, go to 145.

162

As you step off the pavement a screech of tyres heralds the rapid and dangerously erratic approach of a large black BMW. You stand transfixed as it accelerates towards you on the wrong side of the road. At the last moment you manage to throw yourself to one side . . . but it's too late. You bounce off the car bonnet and that's the last you rememeber . . .

When you awake your parents are sitting looking serious by your bedside. You are in hospital. Over next few days as you drift in and out of consciousness, it becomes clear to you that you have been badly injured by a drunken attaché from an African embassy. Unfortunately, not only has he claimed diplomatic immunity from prosecution, but he has been recalled to his own country (also leaving behind £4,000 of unpaid parking fines). The Foreign Office is unwilling to cause a fuss because of a current large arms deal which might be jeopardized by any 'unpleasantness'. This makes suing for compensation almost impossible. Even worse, the manuscript of *Blowing Up Britain* has disappeared and you have to repay the advance to your publisher, Hale & Hearty, as well as legal costs for your unsuccessful civil action.

Your absence from London during your long convalescence in Drabworthy loses you all your professional credibility. If you want to try to start again, you could invest what money you've got in a motorbike and become a despatch rider at 3. If you want to give it all up, then you find yourself stuck on the dole in Drabworthy, a victim of blind fate, brought low by chance, a ruthless God and a quart of Chivas Regal in a flashy car.

163

The show is OK, not much more than that. Exhaustive post-production research (i.e. conversations with a few randomly chosen friends) indicates that your image may have been a serious stumbling block. There are so many young Londoners on the box these days that you had little stand-out appeal. You came across a bit like a poor man's Jonathan Ross. Since there is already a moderately well-off man's Mr Ross, this is something of a disaster. Your career in television lasts all of three weeks before the plug is pulled on your show. Friends who had been thrilled and envious at the prospect of your stardom are now embarrassed by your failure. You retreat to Drabworthy; not so much a has-been as a never-really-was. ☠

164

You take a long weekend in Somerset to produce some ideas. You know that the simplicity of the countryside will clear your mind, so you've borrowed Vanessa's cottage at Combe Dancing, and her Porsche to get down there. You begin to feel creative as you cruise at 95 mph on the M4, Dire Straits playing on the CD. After twelve hours of closely studying videos while relaxing in the jacuzzi you think you've got something. After dinner at Spotprice, the restaurant in the village (two stars in Michelin), you're sure of it. You open a bottle of Pol Roger to celebrate.

It's so brilliant and so obvious you can't imagine why you didn't think of it before: you, Tim Tryer, should host the show. And you even have a name for it – *The Tim Tryer Show*.

Here you feel you have struck a great truth – fortune (and fame) favours the brave. The way to success is through blinding confidence in your own genius. Convince yourself of it and you can convince Vanessa and the money man NICK LEASEBACK that you were born to do this show. But how confident do you feel?

At this point, think of a number between 1 and 10, double it and add your age. Then add today's date for luck. If the total is more than 60, go to 170. If not, 130.

165

The general staff seem to do themselves pretty well these days! A quick calculation of the cost of whisky circulating at the MoD party produces a sum approaching that of a nearly new Exocet in the international arms market. Four trebles later you unsteadily extricate yourself from a monologue of terrorist anecdotes by a brigadier and regain a (by now) deserted Whitehall. Go to 127.

166

When you get home that night you are furious with yourself. You had a once-in-a-lifetime chance of sleeping with one of the most beautiful girls in London and you threw it away. You'll never get anywhere if you never take risks. You go to sleep in despair.

But things cheer up in the morning. At eight the phone rings. It's Rose. 'I'm sorry I'm calling so early. I hope I didn't wake you.'

'It's OK, I was wide awake,' you lie.

'Oh good. It's just that I've just had a call from the office. Apparently Joan Collins and Peter Ustinov have both said that they won't be able to make it to the show tonight. We're desperately trying to find some other guests. I don't suppose you'd be interested. It would really get me out of trouble if you could do it.'

Amazingly enough your diary turns out to be empty. You generously agree to give the BBC an hour or so of your time.

'Oh super,' says Rose. 'Let's have lunch. I want to know everything about you. You know, for Terry's questions . . .'

Lunch would be no problem. Things are looking great again. You've got the telly tonight and all lunch to continue your campaign on Rose. Brilliant. Turn to 78.

167

Your elevation to the inner ranks of London's young social elite, plus your involvement in the rock biz, do wonders for your prestige. Your flatmates are hugely impressed by your success and the free tickets which you are now able to distribute.

The bad news is that it takes you no more than a couple of weeks to see that The Idle Rich are exactly what their name implies. They simply don't have the energy to get their act together. So although you have no trouble in finding a record deal, it is quite impossible to get the group to do any of the work required by it. Despite the satisfaction of a brief affair with Miranda Mountebank, you find the experience unrewarding. And there's worse to come. The record company demand their money back and, since you've delivered nothing to them, you have little choice but to comply. When you look into the small print you discover that you are responsible for all the money that has been wasted on rehearsal halls that went unused, instruments that have yet to be played and photographs that were never taken. And the strain of keeping up with the social habits of your clients has taken a heavy toll. You are just able to pay off your debts, but it costs you all your money.

Go home and lick your wounds at 129.

168

You can practically feel the stinking breath of the hooligans on your neck when you decide to drop your case and your typewriter. You even throw away your wallet in the hope that it will be a distraction. Your belongings fall to the pavement, slowing the gang down and giving you a vital half-second's advantage. Now that you're not weighed down you can really run, your fear sends adrenalin pumping through your system and gives you a speed you never knew you possessed. Blood pounds in your temples, your heart and lungs must surely burst at any moment, but if you can just keep going you may yet make it.

Behind you the hooligans are beginning to give up the chase. They've drunk far too much, they can feel the fags in their lungs and the curry in their guts. And anyway, you're small beer and hardly worth the effort. They stop running and half-heartedly meander back up the road to see if there's anything in your suitcase worth ripping off.

With an inexpressible sense of relief you sense that the danger is passed. You look back over your shoulder to check that all is well and see that the Blue Moon Defectives have turned away from you. If only you had not turned your head just then. If you had been looking in front of you, you would surely have seen the fresh, moist heap of doggy-dos dropped by a prominent Kensington poodle just a few minutes ago and now lying directly in your path. You are still moving at quite a pace when your left foot scores a direct hit on the foul brown pile. With a sickening squelch you lose your grip, power-slide across the pavement and career head-first into a concrete lamppost. You have just enough time to hear a terrible crack before the lights go out. You wake up at 57.

169

Life for the next few months is extremely exciting. At the BBC there are always lots of meetings to ensure that everyone contributes their utmost to the product. You feel you are part of great, unstoppable enterprise. Your administrative workload is high as Peter's assistant, but you feel it'll be worth it when the project is properly off the ground and the shooting begins.

Six months later the meetings are still going on and no date has been set for shooting. You still feel part of an enormous enterprise, but you begin to doubt whether programmes are more than an irritating by-product of the real business of bureaucracy and infighting.

Another six months and still nothing has happened, nothing has been settled. But you are not as worried as you once were. You've started to become part of the organization, and have begun a few small feuds yourself. The nuances in memo writing now fascinate you and most of your free time is spent gossiping about other employees of the BBC: power-shifts in Light Entertainment; falls from grace in News and Current Affairs; sideways promotions in Drama.

The 20-part *History of Sex* is eventually made four years later; on the way it has been transformed into a three-part series on furniture repair. Peter Punchline's fall from grace doesn't affect you, however, since you've managed to attach yourself to another producer. This one is working on a programme on Waterloo – the bi-centenary comes up in 2015. So there's plenty of time for memos, meetings, manipulation . . .

Congratulations, you're a company man. But FAME AND FORTUNE did not lie this way. ☠

170

Yes, you can do it! You've come through a lot since you arrived in London, but now you have enough blinding egotism and confidence to take your bosses' breath away. When you present yourself to them on Monday morning, they are bowled over by your conviction in your own destiny. They agree to everything you suggest – except one thing – the name of the programme. They want to hedge their bets by calling it *Idol Chatter*, rather than *Tim Tryer*. You throw a tantrum and severely damage an Alexander Calder mobile in Leaseback's office, but it's all contrived, you know you'll give in now that they've conceded the main point.

There are three weeks to the pilot transmission so you throw yourself into preparation. Go to 178.

171

Two hours later you are sitting at the best table in the city's smartest ethnic restaurant, Old School Thai, in Chelsea. It's 10.00 p.m. and you've just finished a bottle of Pol Roger with Vanessa. She smiles at you, then produces a large envelope from her bag and gives it to you. It contains a Rolex Oyster wristwatch and a highly lucrative contract made out in your name for a job at Nothing Special. Go to 59.

172

In the taxi into central London, Johnny asks you which set of demonstrators you would rather cover: the Christian Purity League or the Amalgamated Union of British Prostitutes. If you want to march with the vicars go to 49. If you want to streetwalk with the tarts go to 10.

173

Go to bed? Just like that? It's not yet nine o'clock. You'll be wanting mummy to tuck you in next. Get a grip. You can still see Sophie at 138. This is your last chance to redeem yourself. If you're just going to lie self you might as well stop right here. Really – young people nowadays.

It does you no good. Fate has decreed that no matter what you do you are going to be done over. It's just not your lucky night.

You are not fit to go back to work for three weeks. When you do, it is to find that there is no longer a job waiting for you. Everyone is very sympathetic, but the general feeling is that the police don't act without severe provocation and, in any case, gross indecency is not the sort of offence with which any company wants to be associated.

When your case finally comes up it is soon clear that, in the absence of any witnesses in the alley, it is simply your word against the arresting officer's. Juries are always inclined to believe police evidence unless there is overwhelming reason not to. In your case your clean record, the few character witnesses who will endure the embarrassment of a court appearance on your behalf (they all would have turned up if you'd been done for insider dealing, or even drugs, but flashing in an alley . . .) and the clear medical evidence of your physical punishment suffice to temper the charges against you. But they do not remove them entirely. You get off on gross indecency and assaulting a police officer. But you are found guilty of a breach of the peace, fined £250 and bound over.

You leave court with a criminal record, no job, and no prospect of one. You're pretty close to the bottom. If you want to quit and go back to Drabworthy in the hope of starting again one day, no one would blame you. But if you want to carry on, go to 135.

175

The ease with which you take to your new trade does not reflect entirely to your advantage. Is it really such a good thing that you prove so adept at taking councillors to lunch at London's smartest restaurants, pumping them full of brandy and fixing them up with fact-finding visits to Des Res's holiday village developments at Marbella? Are you proud of the skill with which you connive with estate agents to come up with fanciful descriptions of shoddy buildings?

'Major transportation facilities are close at hand,' you write of one new housing estate. It has been built in the patch of waste land between a mainline railway track and a motorway flyover. 'You'll own a penthouse in the sky,' you say to gullible punters about to splash out a quarter of a million on a two-bed in what was, six months before, a condemned council high-rise.

You learn one thing soon enough. You wouldn't want to live in one of the houses you are so brilliant at selling. Despite your employer's generous offer of a reduced rate, you'd rather go it alone. If you want to, go and buy your own home at 46. If not, wait awhile. In the meantime, your career continues at 62.

176

You arrive back at Barchester Gardens to find Jamie Pole-Position winding down from a hard day at De Bono Lizard by doing some trading on his own account. He's selling some gold he picked up cheap in Hong Kong overnight at a substantial profit in New York. His phone is clutched between shoulder and chin. With his left hand he is working a pocket calculator, which provides a constant mathematical commentary to the information he is receiving on the pocket Reuters machine lying on the table in front of him. Next to the Reuters is the business that is occupying his right hand – a mirror, a razor-blade and a small heap of white powder, which he is chopping down to the finest possible consistency.

Jamie looks up at you briefly. 'Hey Tim, what's up? Fancy a toot of God's Dandruff?'

If you fancy sitting down with Jamie and getting high, snort off to 8.

If you want to go straight up to bed in disgust, head up to 173.

177

You throw yourself thoroughly into the piece about left-handers and come up with good material about four prominent sinistral metropolitans:

LAZLO KUNSTWERK, design guru;

TERENCE BROADSHEET, editor of the hi-tech serious daily newspaper, *The Cursor*;

DES RES, an extremely wealthy property developer;

TONY TOT, advertising executive with the *Barfly, Baffle and Tot* agency.

When you come to write the article though, you have a problem: do you carve up your subjects (they certainly gave you enough material for that) and ingratiate yourself with the editor of *Malice*, or do you write a very straight piece in the hope of staying on the right side of these influential people?

If you send them up rotten, go to 76. If you give them an easy ride, go to 131.

178

At the meeting to decide the guests for the first edition of *Idol Chatter*, three selections are presented. Which do you choose:
Isaiah and Irving Berlin, Rupert and Iris Murdoch, 160.
Edward and Samantha Fox, Prince Edward and Prince, 56.
Cilla and Conrad Black, Norman and Peter Scott, 139.

179

Things are going really well. You keep on the flat in Reginald Maudling House as a retail outlet but move to a yuppie compound by the river in Wapping. After three months turnover is up to £150,000 a month and you are supplying a large part of the East End. You now employ three lieutenants who actually do the main business, which is keeping your dealers terrified.

There have been some nasty scenes when you have tried to squeeze in on someone else's patch, but you are resolute in your intention of increasing your market share. An American industrialist said at the turn of the century, 'It's hard to run a steel mill without machine guns,' and you are finding that your business runs much more smoothly when lubricated by the threat of inappropriately severe physical damage.

By the end of the year you are turning over £1 million a month and are planning a coup which will take you up among the big boys in the international narcotics world. However, at this stage a collection of short, swarthy men in dark suits who live in New York but often visit Sicily take an interest in you. This interest expresses itself in the explosion of your Porsche with you inside accompanied by your glossy, page three model mistress. The tabloids runs stories on 'THE LONG BANK HOLIDAY' chronicling your life and times. The violence doesn't end with your demise, however; as a thorough warning to other pushy types they terminate your henchmen, your parents in Drabworthy, your cleaning-lady, your French master from school and someone you met three years ago in a pub.

Lots of fame, lots of fortune. Unfortunately you didn't have enough life to enjoy it. ☠

180

YOU'VE WON!

The first night of *Idol Chatter* is a raging success. Your final choice of guests included Colonel Gaddafi, Bette Midler, Sue Lawley and Ian Botham, but the critics and the public scarcely noticed, since they are overwhelmed with your arrival as an overnight superstar. They adore your redneck intellectual persona, your quirk of calling everyone – male and female – Jimmy, and your occasional grabbing of a guest's lapels and head butt to emphasize a point.

O.K., so the Foreign Office goes crazy when you leave Gaddafi senseless on the studio floor after a particularly vicious butt. The Shi'ite really hits the fan and they claim that the Gulf War is liable to explode into a global conflagration thanks to your brutal approach to diplomacy. But what does that bunch of namby-pamby upper-class pinkos know about diplomacy anyway? As it happens the Big G comes up to you at the after-show party, downs a stiff Sloe Screw Up Against The Wall and says; 'Yo Tim, no sweat. All publicity is good publicity. Am I right or what? Hey, Mazeltov have a nice day.' Or at least that's what his interpreter says he says.

The second week of the show is an even greater sensation: the Beatles re-form with Julian Lennon standing in for his dad. *EastEnders* is squeezed from top place in the TV top ten.

Your life has changed overnight. Suddenly you find yourself unable to nip out for twenty Silk Cut without crowds gathering. Tabloid journalists camp outside your door. Girlfriends from university sell their highly imaginative kiss and tell memoirs to the downmarket Sunday papers. You acquire an agent REDDY CASH, who renegotiates your salary to £100K a show (renegotiable every three months), a price Affair Corp are happy to pay since they are now showing *Idol Chatter* globally to a weekly audience of 100 million. You appear on the cover of *Newsweek*,

Time, Vogue, The Face, Tatler, Malice, Aquarist Monthly, Practical Beekeeping . . .

And it's not just major interviews either. You are soon forced to employ a staff of three just to make up answers to the silly questions newspaper style sections want to ask you. In any one week you are liable to face inquiries about what you keep in your desk, bathroom cabinet, bedside table, refrigerator, glove compartment and posing pouch. They want to know about your favourite designers, colours, foods, drinks and marsupials. What are you giving your Mum for Christmas? Which is your favourite room? How do you spend the day? What do you wish you'd known at 18? What do you wish you'd never known at all?

After a while this incessant attention begins to become boring. So you start playing games with the media. You tell three interior design magazines and a brace of colour supplements that they can each have the exclusive rights to photograph you at home in the vast Georgian mansion you have bought for yourself outside Ascot (it quite overshadows Andrew and Fergie's little place, one need hardly say). Of course the photographers and journalists all arrive at the same time, so you insist that they fight one another for the privilege of the story on a winner-takes-all basis. The result makes an entertaining little video for showing your guests after dinner and it only makes the magazines – who love to be treated rough – even more desperate for access to you.

Then there's the question of women. Naturally you deny all the rumours linking you to a certain Well-Known Unhappy Princess, but they say that you tell a different story in private. And it's really embarrassing how all those models who married rock stars decide that they made the wrong decision and come chasing after you. After all, do you really want to have to spend all day on the phone telling Mick and Bruce and the boys that it actually wasn't your fault. When Madonna dedicates her new album to you, it becomes clear that you have become the media sensation of the age; the winner of the 20th century.

You've cracked it at last: fame, wealth and beautiful lovers. Of course you still have problems; but they're much more *interesting* problems . . .